To my Core and Super Memories
I love you,
Verdayle

Hope's Garden

Verdayle

Order this book online at www.trafford.com/08-0728
or email orders@trafford.com

Most Trafford titles are also available at major online book retailers.

© Copyright 2008 Verdayle Forgét.
Illustrated by Verdayle Forgét.
Cover Design/Artwork by Verdayle Forgét.
All rights reserved. No part of this publication may be reproduced, stored in a retrieval system, or transmitted, in any form or by any means, electronic, mechanical, photocopying, recording, or otherwise, without the written prior permission of the author.

Note for Librarians: A cataloguing record for this book is available from Library and Archives Canada at www.collectionscanada.ca/amicus/index-e.html

Printed in Victoria, BC, Canada.

ISBN: 978-1-4251-8019-5

We at Trafford believe that it is the responsibility of us all, as both individuals and corporations, to make choices that are environmentally and socially sound. You, in turn, are supporting this responsible conduct each time you purchase a Trafford book, or make use of our publishing services. To find out how you are helping, please visit www.trafford.com/responsiblepublishing.html

Our mission is to efficiently provide the world's finest, most comprehensive book publishing service, enabling every author to experience success. To find out how to publish your book, your way, and have it available worldwide, visit us online at www.trafford.com/10510

 www.trafford.com

North America & international
toll-free: 1 888 232 4444 (USA & Canada)
phone: 250 383 6864 ♦ fax: 250 383 6804 ♦ email: info@trafford.com

The United Kingdom & Europe
phone: +44 (0)1865 722 113 ♦ local rate: 0845 230 9601
facsimile: +44 (0)1865 722 868 ♦ email: info.uk@trafford.com

10 9 8 7 6 5 4 3 2 1

IN MEMORIAM

To Dixie (Emma Lou) Berry

ACKNOWLEDGEMENTS

When this story first began to fester in my mind Barbara Johnston (B.J.) was the first to propel me forward. With her experience as a writer and as a PBS Emmy Award winner I took her seriously as many long distant phone calls bolstered my confidence.

Despite relentless hounding from clients and friends I have stubbornly avoided the Tech World. The Isaacs family loaned me the needed computer and their patience never wavered despite their many interventions when Mac and I could not come to terms with each other. They encouraged and fed me through many frustrations.

Great thanks to Kerry Dalton for taking the time from the hectic days before opening race day to work on the back cover and for all of the enthusiasm along the way.

To all of those that read the many revised versions of the manuscript, thank you for all of your feedback.

PROLOGUE

It was a soft Seattle rain, the kind that seems wetter somehow, a cold fuzz seeping into the marrow. We drove through the city in silence. At the bottom of the hill I told him to turn left onto the street running parallel to the freeway viaduct.

"There it is," I pointed. "Stop the car."

"I don't like this one bit," he said under his breath.

"We have had this conversation. Just stay in the car, I'll be right back."

"No, we didn't have a conversation. You coerced me." His grumble was almost a groan.

I stepped from the pristine safety of the car. Figures scattered like frightened rats in the glare of the headlights. The putrid stench of rotting spirits closed my throat. I swallowed back the urge to turn back to the car, but entered the black hole under the freeway where there are no reflections. I waited for my pupils to dilate and focus on shadows within shadows.

I began the scavenger hunt, watching my manicured fingernails dig through wet editions of last weeks news, black trash bags and discarded wine bottles and food wrappers.

Placed behind the overflowing dumpster was the large cardboard box that would become my motel room for the night. At one time it held a brand new refrigerator. With fear and caution I pulled it out from the debris and stepped back to look at my prize. Suddenly the box moved with a thumping sound. Startled, I screamed and jumped back, expecting to see a wild animal or a family of rats. For a moment it was quiet, then a rustling. Slowly I opened the flaps as a small meow came out of the darkness inside the box. Gently and with great apprehension I turned the box on its side and waited. A small-emaciated kitten stuck its little gray head out, looked at me, and ran into the night.

I poked my head into the box. It was clean and dry. I put my backpack inside, wondering why I had kept all these years. As I huddled inside, I looked out from under the flap and stared at the black spit-polished shoes and razor sharp creased pant legs that were eye level to me. The laces on his shoes were tied with exact meticulous bows on both feet.

"Will you be alright?" His voice echoed above me.

"I'll be fine."

"I hope so. I'll pick you up in the morning," he said.

I stuck my head out of the box and watched him slowly walk through the puddles toward the car. I heard him say under his breath, "The lady is nuts." His white Cadillac pulled away like a ghost in the night chill. I felt the aloneness descend, heavy and foreboding.

For comfort I opened the backpack and ran my hand over the old folded creased brown paper shopping bag, Faded magic marker flowers bloomed on its wrinkled sides. Strange, I thought, the bag is wilted but somehow the flowers remained a never-ending spring. I took out the lovely gray wing feather and stroked its softness across my salty wet cheek.

The sound of the traffic on the freeway above pounded relentlessly on my head. I wrapped the old wool afghan around my shoulders. It was a bittersweet comfort. I pulled it tighter around me, closer like a cocoon. My fingers ran over the knobby pattern and I wondered about the hands that had knitted it. I had never had the heart to put it in the laundry, to wash away its spirit somehow. I smelled the sweetness that had never gone away.

I remembered that it had been a long road in both directions. I hugged my knees and began rocking to the beat of the city. I wouldn't waste the night with sleep. For a moment I closed my eyes. A low purr interjected as I felt the small soft body crawl up my chest and curl up in my neck. I put my cheek on its fur, "I know what you're feeling Kiddo, I was a stray once and someone took me in."

It had been the mid-1970s when the country was knocked on its back and somehow couldn't regain its footing, there didn't seem to be a solid place to stand.

There had been Kent State, Watts, Memphis, Dallas and San Francisco and the day Graceland fell silent. Each broadcast of "Nightly News" brought the war into our homes and we watched real people being killed right before our eyes. The taste of futility was bitter on the public tongue.

A movement began to heave across the country, scooping up the young and the willing in its wake, a narcissistic pilgrimage to self-enlightenment as a whole mass of humanity held two fingers to the sky and vowed their right to the new Declaration of Independence.

God had died. Flowers were placed in headbands and upon the altars of new gods rising to the top. Dylan, Joplin, The Grateful Dead all shared the worship of the multitudes. Peace, free speech, free love, free expression, New Age religion and drugs became the new mantra.

The government, patriotism, responsibility, authority and the establishment fell from grace and The Me Generation was born. Accountability was tossed to the wind as doing our own thing came to pass.

I unwrapped my tuna sandwich and opened the thermos of coffee. I gave the kitten some of the tuna and it ate like it had never had eaten before. I put the little body under the afghan and it snuggled into my armpit; our bond had been sealed.

In spite of the layers of a turtleneck, sweater and the old parka a shiver ran up my spine. The wool sox and fleece lined boots were a meager deterrent to the dampness. No amount of outer garments could stave off the chill of the fear of remembering. I curled up, trying to make myself smaller. I knew I had to come back just one more time.

Long after they are vacated, old abandoned houses at least have signs of life once lived; clean squares on the walls where pictures once hung, scuff marks on bare wood floors left by children's feet, a dark soot covered fireplace, the remnant of cozy fires and Christmas stockings. Outside, unattended rose bushes rise above weeds and manage to bloom somehow, in spite of themselves.

There was no one here, not a sign of a population that once filled this darkness; not a scrap of anything familiar remained. All had moved on, abandoning this small community without a trace of what had happened here.

PART ONE

It was nearly midnight when the bus pulled into the Seattle Greyhound Bus Depot. Three days before I had taken claim to the back seat of the bus, not wanting to hear anyone's story and not wanting to be questioned about mine.

The bus was full, having picked up passengers as it moved west. I was the last one off and followed the rest into the depot. There were hugs, kisses and laughter as grandparents scooped up grandchildren. Off to the side where passengers were waiting to load the bus, good-byes were exchanged with hugs, kisses and tears. Grandparents reluctantly let go of grandchildren.

I went into the bathroom and splashed hot water on my face; the mirror reflected an aged version of myself.

I found a bench along the wall and sat down. When the passengers left and it was quiet I folded my jacket, put it under my head and went to sleep. It seemed like only moments when I felt someone tapping me on the shoulder. I opened my eyes and the ticket agent was standing over me. "I'm sorry, but you can't stay here any longer," he said in a kind voice.

It was morning and the sun was shining through the windows. He gave me a forced smile and handed me a five-dollar bill. "Buy yourself a nice breakfast.

"I don't want your money, thanks anyway."

He folded the bill and with a sad look in his eyes he laid it on the bench beside me, turned and walked away.

I tied the sleeves of my jacket around my waist, picked up my backpack and left the building. I walked down to Stewart Street and started going south on 4th Ave. I could see the skyscrapers raising up from the heart of the city. I quickly learned that the north-south streets were level and the east-west streets were steep hills going down to the waterfront.

The heat was choking me. Everything I owned, all I had left, was in the backpack that was blistering my shoulders. The July heat absorbed in the concrete came up and hit me in the face. I thought I was going to be sick. In the doorway of an office building I sat down in the shade feeling my heart beating in my feet.

Well-dressed ladies went in and out of the building. I didn't look at them directly and they didn't look at me at all.

Someone in sparkling Alligator shoes was standing over me. I didn't look at his face when he screamed, "Get! Go on, you can't park here," Like yelling at a mutt lost in a pedigree neighborhood.

I had walked for hours in the canyon of the buildings. There had been a plan, I would find a low-cost motel or the YWCA and begin job-hunting right away. 'Best laid plans,' I sighed.

It was clear by the doorman at the Olympic Hotel that

I was uptown and far removed from my price range. I went back north to Union Street, turned west and descended the hills toward the water. At last, I got to 1st Ave. I let the smell and breeze of Puget Sound wash over me.

My options seemed to have come to a dead end as I crossed the street to Waterfront Park and sat on a bench facing the water. Once again I was invisible as tourists in white shorts with pink ice cream cones in their hands and cameras around their necks strolled past me. I put the backpack under my head, hung my throbbing feet over the end of the bench and closed my eyes. The sound of seagulls lulled me into a false sensation of peace.

Suddenly I heard someone yell, "Hey!" I opened one eye, then the other, just to make sure I wasn't dreaming. She stood at the end of the bench wearing red boxer shorts, a purple T-shirt and a huge straw hat about the size of an umbrella. The brim and crown were covered in bright multi-colored plastic flowers, the weight making the edges of the brim droop to cover her face. She looked like some bizarre mushroom from another planet or Disneyland refugee. I heard myself laughing, a sound that I had not heard for a very long time.

"You're new around here aren't ya?" She snapped.

"How do you know that?"

"Not real hard to figure that out, not many people around here wear boots and have a parka under their butt in the middle of summer. I also know almost everything that goes on and if you were from around here you never would have laughed at me."

"Sorry, it's the hat, it surprised me. I didn't mean any offense."

"It's my garden. No matter where I go I take beauty with me. Where are you going?"

"I don't know."

"You look like you could use some coffee or something. Come on, let's do lunch."

I got up and limped across the street with her. We found a coffee shop and I followed her through the door. She acted like she owned the place as she squared her shoulders and looked around the room. We sat down in a booth that had not been cleared of dishes.

"Help yourself," she said between bites, "It's been paid for."

I ate some cold French fries and realized I hadn't known how hungry I was. I resisted the urge to shove them into my mouth with both hands. The waitress stood for a moment watching then cleared away the now empty plates.

"We will have two coffees with lots of creamers and sugars," the voice under the hat said.

I looked around the room and noticed that everyone was smiling, not a smile of scorn but a tender smile. I felt myself relax and didn't feel so conspicuous.

The waitress returned with the coffee and two soup bowls with the mountains of creamers and little packets of sugar. She then put a piece of pie down in front of each of us. "The pie is my treat. The hat, very cool."

We ate our pie and drank our coffee in silence. The noise

began to subside as people ended their lunch hour.

"What's your name, where are you from?" I wanted to start a conversation.

"Around here no one has a name and no one has a history, we pick a name that suits us for today. Everyone calls me Posy."

I smiled, "That's a perfect choice. I never thought of changing my name, it just suits me, so I guess I'll keep going with it. It has always been a neon sign on my life."

"What is it?"

"Hope." I said, wondering if I had any left.

"That's a good name, how old are you?"

"Nineteen, how about yourself?"

"I'm older, early twenties. I really don't want to talk about this anymore. I prefer to live in the moment." She began to construct a tower with the cream containers.

The waitress picked up the plates and put the check face-down on the table. I turned it over. Total charge, twenty cents with a large "Thank You" and a smiley face. Posy took a red tulip off of her hat and laid it across the bill, "Gotta leave a tip," she smiled. I added a quarter.

Out on the scorching sidewalk again we stood in uncomfortable silence, neither of us knowing what to do next. I felt my feet begin to poach,

"Do you have a place to stay?" She broke the tension.

"No."

"You're welcome to stay at my place for a day or two, but you need to know up front, there will be no drugs, no booze and no sex. If that doesn't work for you, just lay it on the line right now."

"That more than works for me, I appreciate it very much." I felt relief and apprehension all at the same time. My options were a bit limited.

We walked along the waterfront without talking. Not far from the ferry dock she turned into an old brick building and went up the splintered stairs. I followed without question. There was nothing to ask. It wasn't that I trusted, but I needed to land somewhere, if only for a moment. I knew I would know when it was time to leave, I always did.

The hall was dark and narrow. Two bare light bulbs hanging from flimsy cords from the ceiling made a futile attempt to illuminate the vanishing point. The air was stagnant with the smells of several dinners cooking, all indistinguishable.

"Welcome to the Plaza." She unlocked the door and we stepped inside.

There was one friendly room with a large window overlooking the street and the waterfront. The mattress on the floor was covered with flowered sheets, worn but clean. There were no chairs, no couch, and no refrigerator. Beside the mattress was an upside-down cardboard box covered with floral wallpaper. In one corner of the room there were bricks on the floor on top of which were a hotplate and two small pots. Beside the bricks another box, painted white, and lying on edge, contained a few plates, cups and some silverware. Inside three other white-painted boxes her clothes rested neatly folded. It was amazing to me how she had made a home out of almost nothing. She even managed to have a few books and an ivy plant growing in the window.

"Well?" She asked, watching me take inventory. She opened the window and a puff of refreshing salt air entered the room. "It's the view that sold me."

"Very impressive. Do you have a bathroom?"

She pointed to the only door. I opened it and looked up to the ceiling and said inside my head, "Thank you, God." She also had a bathtub.

I came back into the room and saw her sitting on the floor leaning against the mattress. For the first time she was hatless. Her long hair hung in waves, gold and gleaming. She looked small and vulnerable without the large power emblem on her head. She was stunning in a fragile sort of way.

She put her hand on the mattress. "Sit. Relax."

I sat down and put my backpack safely between my feet. I wanted to melt into the flowers.

Suddenly she sprang to her feet and took charge. She emptied her pockets, pulling out catsup packets, half-and-half containers, packets of sugar, crackers and red-and-white mints. She went into the bathroom and put some water into one of the pots, added the catsup and half-and-half.

As it began to heat on the hot plate I mustered my nerve. "Do you mind if I soak in your tub?"

"Help yourself, be careful with the soap though. I have to go clear uptown to one of those fancy hotels to get it.

"What? Why? How do you do that?"

"Easy, no problem. Walk in; go down the hall when the

maids are cleaning first thing in the morning. There's all kinds of stuff on their carts, shampoo, lotion, soap and sometimes even ballpoint pens."

"Isn't that stealing?"

"Money is stealing, soap is maintenance." She said giving an indignant wave of her hand.

I didn't have it in me to start a moral argument; it was none of my business anyway.

I closed the bathroom door and turned on the tap of the bathtub. The water wasn't scalding like I like it, but I didn't care at that point.

Slowly I unlaced my boots. Tears shot out of my eyes as I took them off. The blisters had broken and skin was stuck to my socks. My clothes fell to the floor and I sank into the water up to my neck. I took the wrapper off the little soap and noticed the same name on the huge white towel folded neatly on the back of the john. Maintenance for sure, I smiled.

The water pulled every emotion, every last drop of energy out of me like a huge poultice.

I thought of my mama and how she always had those little bath-oil beads that smelled like lilac. The tears ran down my cheeks and made little circles in the water. I watched in abstract detachment.

The water began to cool. I stepped out of the tub exhausted and defused. I hugged the thick terry cloth towel like an old friendly teddy bear.

Dressed, except for my socks and boots, I opened the door. She handed me a cup of soup and a packet of crackers. Nothing had ever tasted better. She must have sensed my depletion and gave me the gift of silence. I finished the soup, fell back onto the flowered sheets and slid over the line into sleep.

The light from the window was relentless. I sat up like a rocket before I opened my eyes. I didn't know where I was for a moment. I shook the fuzz out of my head and looked around the room. She was gone. The clock on the cardboard box end table said six o'clock; a.m. I realized I was all-alone.

Panic gripped my ribs and squeezed, I could hardly breathe. My backpack, where's my backpack, I thought I was screaming but no sound came out. I rolled off the mattress and bumped my head on the edge of it. Quickly I opened the zipper and was checking the contents when the door opened and she flew in and threw me an orange.

"Good morning. Everything there?"

"Yeah. Where do you get your energy, not to mention your attitude?"

"That's all life is, attitude, and by the way, I don't care what's in your bag. Your stuff is of no interest to me, o.k."

"I don't just trust at first sight."

"You shouldn't, it's a crazy world out there."

"Where have you been, if you don't mind me asking."

"Don't mind, I've been working. I have a paper route. I have a friend that loans me his bike. The pay stinks but it's something that gets me by and I have all day to do my real work."

"Which is?"

She took off her hat and shook out her hair. "I'm sort of a people person, I'll take you with me tomorrow if you want."

"I'd like that."

I looked out the window at the mass of movement below. Ships waited to be loaded or unloaded. Boats left a wake of salt spray behind them as they raced toward the horizon. Trains moved through the scene and specks of moving humanity changed the colors of the picture. Everyone had a promise to keep. Without a promise, is there a point, I wondered as I turned with a heavy sigh?

Posy was standing behind me, "If you aren't in any hurry to expand your horizons you can hang out here for awhile, no obligation. You're free to leave anytime with no hard feelings."

"Thanks. It's worth a try to see how it goes. I plan to get a job. In the mean time I have a few dollars that I can contribute. I pay my own way. I'm not beholden to anyone."

"O.K." She raised her hand and one thumb.

I entered the academics of Street Wise and my instructor was a master. The world as I knew it had taken a drastic twist, throwing my life into foreign territory. Kansas was as but a brief memory and becoming less familiar every day. There wasn't a smell, sound, or experience that came from my Midwest background. I had been pulled up by the roots from the sandy soil and transplanted in cement. But weeds, they say, will find a crack and grow, in spite of themselves.

Posy loved the Public Market. It was the hub of her wheel. Everyone knew her. Vendors' faces would light up as they called her name. They gave her fruits, vegetables, and loaves of bread, and sometimes a salmon, too small for a quick sell. She created Christmas and The Fourth of July all at once. Even little children reached out their arms to her and would giggle at her hat. For me, it was better then when the carnival had come to town. The smells, colors, and people were a delicious concoction.

With arms full of overflowing bags containing the bounty from the vendors we would go back to the room to sort and rebag the produce into smaller bags. For us, she would set aside two of each.

The first time we did this, I had no clue what we were doing or where we were going. She didn't explain and I didn't ask. "Let's go to work," was all she said. We put the small bags into the big bags and I followed her out the door.

Under the viaduct, across the street from the docks, was a forgotten unseen city, a portable society. I felt my legs turn to rubber, as we got closer. All I could see were shapes slinking deep into the darkness. It felt as if I had been picked up and thrown into a third world country where I didn't know the language or the customs. Out in the sunlight, on the shadows edge an old man, unshaven in dirty bib overalls, walked past pushing a shopping cart full of clothing, blankets and a pair of worn shoes. He didn't acknowledge anyone. He continued to look down, found his place and sat on the curb and picked at the dirty threads hanging from the rolled up pant cuffs.

Who were these people and more importantly, why was I here? This wasn't a movie or TV.

We crossed the street and stepped into the shade of the freeway above. I hung back, not knowing what to expect. I felt the blood begin to pound in my head as fear gripped me like a vice. But again, instantly, Posy brought magic, hellos and high fives. I began to breathe again.

"Hey Flash, what ya got?" She called out to a young man with a grin as wide as Puget Sound.

"I got time, what do you have?"

"I have good looks and a new friend."

"I got a deck of cards, I'll trade ya for whatever's in that sack."

"Deal." She handed him a bag and he pulled out an orange and grinned again.

"Where's Auntie Bea?"

Flash pointed to a woman on our right and said to me, "They say she's crazy, but she doesn't care what the outsiders think. To the folks here she is known as The Deacon."

She was sitting in a broken lawn chair; by contrast her posture was strong and proud. She was singing "Amazing Grace," and with several people swaying around her, humming with the chorus, her eyes would drift away and close. She was clearly alone in a place where no one could enter. Something in her voice was hypnotic as she glided from a guttural power to a soft honey whisper.

On her head she wore a purple turban that matched her flowing, loose fitting, long dress. She wasn't wearing shoes. Her skin had the sheen of melting milk chocolate. When she saw Posy she went from, "how sweet the sound" to "Hey girl, where you been if you don't mind my askin'?"

"Well, I do mind' Posy laughed and gave her a long warm hug and a kiss on the cheek. "I want you to meet my new friend Hope, she's new in town and is staying with me for a while."

"Come over here child, let me see you."

I walked slowly and stood in front of her. Her eyes were clear and sharp as they held my gaze with their softness and wisdom. She seemed to be reading me like a book to which only she knew the ending. After a long pause, she smiled and said, "Nice to meet you."

Respectfully every one moved away, giving us room. Posy gave each of them a bag and handed one to Auntie Bea, "I saved the best for last."

"You're a good girl." Auntie Bea put the bag under her chair. "I'll save it for later."

"Did you know that I used to sing with Bessie Smith? I met Muddy Waters once. Those were high times back then." Her memories brought a far away sweetness to her eyes.

Off in the distance someone began playing "Just A Closer Walk With Thee" on a harmonica, slow and low. I could see her brown toes began to tap as she waved him to come to her. Like a Pied Piper he led the others in bringing up the harmony.

As the rhythm began to build, she belted out the melody loud and strong. We listened to music and the stories she told of the clubs in Chicago's South Side, the Juke Joints down South and Jazz played on porches on hot summer nights in

Georgia. Every one had a memory, if not their finest hour, for now they knew they were close to a shining star. No matter how many times they had heard the stories, they still listened intently. Some of them stayed at a shelter at night and came to be with friends during the day. Others didn't want to leave, making makeshift homes out of whatever they could scrape together to build flimsy structures to contain themselves and their meager belongings.

At last Auntie Bea leaned back in her chair and said, "Ya'll scoot now and let an old lady get some rest."

The sun was going down and the light was beginning to dim. We walked in silence to the pier and watched the last rays of the sun duck behind the mountains as the water of Puget Sound took on a pink blush. I couldn't remember a more luscious day.

This was the precedent for the days to come. While Posy delivered the papers, I had time to myself. I would splash water on my face, boil the coffee grounds again and make the bed.

On the floor I would take my secret out of my backpack; a sketchbook, pencils, a small pencil sharpener and a ball point pen. I was learning to draw smaller, not to use paper unwisely. Other secrets hid in the dark corners. I always put everything back into the backpack in exactly the same place. It was a small thing, but it was the only thing that I could truly call mine.

I counted the bills, kept back five dollars and returned the rest to the bottom. I had no plan to spend the money unless to buy something essential, I just wanted to reach into my pocket and feel it there sometimes.

At the bottom, in the corner, was the photo I had ripped out of my scrapbook on my way out the door that awful night. The sound of my mother crying and begging me to stay came back like a radio that couldn't be shut off. I leaned closer to the photo so I could better see the details. I covered the eyes of the woman in the picture and looked at the smile, glued on as if it belonged to someone else. Then I covered the smile and focused on the eyes, two dark dead pits, vacant, without the slightest glimmer of life. They weren't looking at the camera, but beyond it at something far away. I looked at her face remembering that it had been a good day when that picture was taken. I remembered because there were so few good days. The river was low that July, shallow enough for wading. We had a picnic with fried chicken and my stepfather had not brought beer for a change.

As I looked at the photo I wondered who this woman had been in her youth. She was a beauty, well educated and full of sparkle, but what were her dreams? What kind of friend had she been? How did she cope when my father walked away when he found out she was pregnant with me because he was a career Army man and didn't want children. When did she settle and sell out?

"I tried to make it better, Mama," I whispered to her image on the paper, "but I never knew how." Then I put her back in the dark.

Sometimes the hole in my heart was so big it almost swallowed me. Posy's effervescence wasn't there to distract me so I went down to the street to watch people moving about. Walking without purpose, I found myself under the viaduct looking for Auntie Bea. She smiled when she saw me. That was what I had been looking for, someone that recognized me and was happy to see me.

"Well land sakes child, what are you doin' in this neck of the woods? Sit down and talk to me awhile."

"I was hungry for a friendly face."

"Tell me about yourself," she said looking at me sideways.

"I would rather listen to you, I'm sure your story has more interest than mine." I sat down on the ground and looked around at the people's spirits melting in the heat.

"Where are you from Auntie Bea?"

"Chicago."

"What are you doing way up here?"

"It's a long story."

"I have nothing but time." I wrapped my arms around my knees.

"Well, my son joined the Army to get us out of the projects. Such a good boy. Every month he sent money home with a note, 'Put this in the jar, Mama, it's our ticket out of hell.' Then he had to go to war and the Army people sent the money and I wasn't able to hear from him very often. Then one month the money didn't come. One day the man in a uniform came to the door and gave me this," she reached into a box under her chair and handed me a small box. Inside was the Purple Heart.

Her eyes welled up with tears. "The man said he was a hero, said he was missing, said his whole platoon had been wiped out. He never came home. Something broke in me that day. I just wanted the bus to take me as far away as I could get." She trailed off and began to hum, holding the heart to her own.

We were quiet for a while. When she opened her eyes, she wiped the tears, blew her nose and regained the proud elegance and grace that was never far away. I found the courage to ask, "What was it like when you were a child?"

"Oh I had a wonderful childhood, just wonderful. My mama Ella, and daddy John, worked for a white family in the big house up on the hill. They owned the big general store on Main Street. It was white-washed stone on the outside and no matter how hot the summer, it was always cool inside. The store would stay open on Friday nights so us colored could shop for goods. Daddy would take the flat-back wagon so we could carry supplies. He would let me hold the reins but I think that old horse knew his way to town. He would just trot down the road with his ears up and the reins loose.

"I loved that store and thought it a magical place. The big red chest by the front door was always full of ice and bottles of cold Coca-Cola. The first thing I would do when I walked in the door is to take a deep breath and smell the coffee in the gunny sacks on the floor. It was sold by the scoop. The same with flour and sugar. Wooden barrels were full of every size of nails. Bolts of bright cloth covered the counter. Mule harnesses and wagon wheels hung from the ceiling. There were big glass jars full of hard candy that only cost a penny a piece. My favorite was horehound drops. Daddy would give me a dime to buy anything I wanted. I felt so grown up to be doin my own shoppin.

"They had lots of land. My mama kept the house and took care of their two children, Emma and Leonard. Daddy kept the grounds, the orchard, and anything that needed fixin' around the place. There was a small house back of the pecan orchard where we lived. He always gave me the peaches and pecans that fell on the ground. Daddy and the Mister hunted together and the Missus and mama worked together in the garden. They laughed when the Missus called mama her black sister.

Emma was close to my age and Leonard was a bit older. They'd rather play with the colored kids, said we were more fun. Emma had lots of books and let me look at them, she told me she would teach me to read someday. I spent hours on those pages tryin to make sense of the words. She had long bright red hair and I would braid it so she could have pigtails like mine, I wished my hair could be so fine. She was taller than the rest of us children and with that hair that made her head look like it was on fire, I could spot her comin' way down the road. We traded chewing gum. We were best friends. We didn't know any different. One day Emma asked my mama, 'Ella, why can't Bea have supper with us in the dinning room?'

"'Because, that's just the way it is, wouldn't be proper.'

"Emma started to cry and I didn't understand. Mama, Daddy, and I always ate supper in the kitchen, and then she would do up the dishes before we went to our house for the night. Oh how I loved that kitchen with the big wood stove and the smell of corn bread and fried okra. On Sunday Mama made ham, red-eye gravy and grits. The salad came right out of the garden. Sunday was church day and I loved to sing for the Lord. Emma wanted to go to our church because it was lively. She would say, "God can sure hear you when ya all shout, 'Praise The Lord', I'm not sure He can hear us, we have to be so quiet.'"

"Did the white kids pick on Emma and Leonard for playing with you and the other black children?"

"Sometimes, but they didn't pay them any mind. It was easier when we were little because it was just the four of us. Leonard, being the only boy, didn't much like being around us girls so he made friends with a colored boy down the road. They went everywhere together for years. Then when Leonard turned eighteen, Willard said to Leonard, 'I can't call you Leno anymore. You're a man now, I gotta call you Mister Leonard,' It broke Leonard's heart and the friendship was never the same. The line was drawn and that's just the way it was."

"What about you and Emma?"

Tears came to her eyes. She folded her hands on her lap, took a deep breath and said, "By now we were no longer considered children. Leonard joined the service and Emma was sent to a girl's school in Atlanta. I remember standing in the middle of the road watching her car being swallowed up by the dust until I couldn't see it anymore. She was slumped in the back seat like a sack of spuds. I spent two days crying in the wood shed. No one came to fetch me. I didn't know how I could bare to live another day.

"I turned sixteen that summer and nothin mattered. I just wanted to dissolve in the heat.

"Then one night when I was lying on my bed I heard Daddy talking in the next room about the Missus' rich sister up in Chicago. Daddy was saying, 'She is a bright girl, there ain't nothin for her here. Things are going to always be the way they always been. I ain't never going to have the same chances as the Mister; him and his got a head start a long time ago. I just as soon live out my day's right where I am. I know my place. No surprises day to day. Anyway, the Mister has always been good to us; far better than most.'

"'The girl is smart, always good with numbers, loving her books, and mercy, can she sing. The Missus' sister could give her work and get her schoolin'. Maybe she has a chance up North. The Missus said they would treat her right. For the sake of the child, John, we have to let her go.'

"Daddy whispered, 'It's so far away, and Chicago is so big.'

"The Missus made the arrangements and bought me a new dress and a new suitcase. Mama made me a sack lunch and took me to the bus station. Daddy wouldn't go. No one had anything to say on the way to town. The Missus drove, lookin straight ahead. Her eyes would well up and she would clear her throat. Mama just looked out the side window.'

"We stood outside the bus station not knowing what to say to each other. I was scared; I had never been more than twenty miles from home. The bus pulled up and people got off and it was time. Mama held me tight. She was crying and she whispered, 'Make us proud, we love you.'

As the bus pulled away I watched mama wave her arms above the dust, lookin as small as I felt. There were about five of us colored at the back of the bus; a family and one fine lookin young man across the aisle from me. We took a shine to each other right off but we were too shy to say anything at first. When the bus made a stop for lunch, the white folks went into the station and I sat on the bench outside and opened my sack to see what was inside. There were ham sandwiches, carrots, fruit, and ginger cake. I was eating a peach when he sat down beside me.

"'Where ya all headed?' He had kind eyes and his voice was deep and soft.

"'Chicago.' That was the only word I could get out.

"'Me too.'"

"We didn't say much. He was a beautiful creature, had arms like tree trunks and a smile that turned me to jelly. I became a woman with just one glance in his direction.

"When we got back on the bus he took a seat beside me. It made me feel safe just having him there. We talked more and more and I liked the way he laughed and made things seem light and not so scary. I didn't think about the end of the road.

"Why was he going to Chicago?"

"His older brother sent him money to come up and be a manager in a Jazz club. His brother said he knew people and if he played his cards right there would be a future for him. We got to know each other in those four days."

"What happened when you got to Chicago?"

"His brother was at the bus depot and so was the new missus, Missus Harvey. Before I left home mama gave me Missus Harvey's phone number, and I gave it to him, never expecting to see him again. He gave me a hug and I went with Missus Harvey.

"She was very friendly as she drove and tried to make me comfortable. I had never seen so many cars all going on the same street. I was nervous but she sensed it and told me we were almost there. When she stopped in front of her house, I couldn't believe it. The street was lined with big trees and the big white house was up a lot of wide steps from the sidewalk. There were flowers everywhere.

"The rooms inside the house were very large with big windows. She took me upstairs to my room. My room, can you believe it? I remember how bright it was with big windows and the walls were yellow.

"I missed Mama and Daddy but Missus Harvey was very kind. Mister Harvey was a lawyer and not home much. I did chores around the house and in the flower beds, which was my favorite."

"Did you ever hear from the man on the bus."?

"Yes. One day, many weeks later, I heard Missus Harvey on the telephone and she was saying, 'Yes, I think that would be just fine. I'm sure she will be happy that you are coming by.'

"When she told me he was coming to see me that afternoon, I felt faint, had to lean up against the wall to keep from falling over. I put on my best dress and watched the clock for the next two hours. I was out on the front porch when he drove up in a big shiny car. He came up the steps all dressed up and smellin like Ivory soap. He sat down beside me and said, 'Hi pretty lady, would you like to go for a spin?'

"He came to see me every Saturday. We would go to a movie or just ride around and listen to the radio in his car. Sometimes I would sing. He loved my voice.

"Many months later, he asked if he could speak with Mister and Missus Harvey alone. He told them he wanted to marry me and they said he would have to ask my mama and daddy. He called them on the spot.

"Then one day he drove down a street and stopped the car in front of a little house. With a big grin on his face he pointed and said, 'so, what do you think of that?'

"It's nice, why?"

"'Well, I'm thinking that could be a good place for us to start our lives, let's go in so you can see if you like it.'

"I was out of the car before he could shut off the motor. The yard was without attention for a long time and the house needed paint. The inside needed fixin' but it was full of possibilities. I gave him a big hug and told him we could make it a home.

"We were married the following summer. Mama and

daddy couldn't come but Mama sent this wonderful afghan that she made." She pulled the afghan out of a plastic bag.

"It's beautiful," I said, touching it lightly.

She took a deep breath and continued. "We moved into the house, had two beautiful baby boys."

"Were you happy?"

"I was happy with Mandy. He was a good man. But I didn't understand the northern ways. There were so many people and they lived so close together, I was used to having space around me. Oh the winter, it was punishing cold. I missed the smell of the red Georgia earth and the pines when it rained. The smell of ripe peaches on the trees could make a mouth water a mile away. There isn't a way to get away from the sweet smell of magnolias hanging on the hot summer air. I never got used to the smell of traffic or Thursdays when it was trash day."

"What were the best times?"

"Sunday chicken, the boys, the neighbors comin' over in an evening and sittin' on the porch. But the best was the rare times I would go with Mandy and sing with the band at the club. I would listen to my voice come out of my mouth and couldn't wait to hear the next note. I'm getting tired, Hope, so I'll just finish. Mandy was shot one night coming out of the club. They said he knew too much about things going on around there, or someone owed him money, I don't know. The police didn't try very hard. I didn't have the money to stay in the house, so Mandy's brother found us a place in the projects. I lost my man and my home all at once, but I had son's to raise so I had to stand tall and go on."

"Why did you come to Seattle rather than going back to Georgia?"

She kicked at a pebble, "I didn't have a home left to go back to. Not long after Mandy and I moved into our house Mrs. Harvey came by and told me my mama had taken sick. She thought I should go down.

"When I got there mama had been moved into the big house, into the Missus room so she could care for mama in the night. The Mister had passed on the year before and daddy tried to keep up on the chores.

"I slept on a cot by mama's bed and spent the days with her. She talked to me about how she had loved her life and how she had been blessed.

"Sometimes I would catch the Missus sitting on the porch crying. She looked so small, like all the life had been sucked out of her, as if she was wasting away along with mama, trying to catch up somehow.

"I sat down beside her. She took my hand in both of hers, 'How can there be a world without Ella, how can the sun continue to rise?' She looked across the yard toward the pine trees. All I could do was nod my head and look with her toward the emptiness.

"Mama gave up in the middle of the night and went home. Her Pastor and Doctor were with us.

"People came by, the faces became a blur as the Missus tried to be the gracious southern hostess.

"It was a beautiful day the afternoon we put her in the

ground. We chose the knoll out by the orchards. In the middle of prayer I opened my eyes and saw Emma on the other side of the grave. She had her head bowed.

"I must have fainted because when I came to Emma was next to me on the ground holding my hand. Someone was holding smelling salts under my nose.

"After mama had been laid to rest everyone went back to the big house to pay respects. Daddy didn't come. I went to our little house to find him. He was sitting at the table still wearing his new suit that didn't hang right on him.

"I didn't speak, I just sat down across from him. His eyes looked like black marbles that didn't move. I left him sittin there all alone, he didn't even know I was there. When I went back later he was asleep on the bed still wearing his suit.

"Emma and I spent the next three days walking the property, retracing our childhood and trying to help her mama and my daddy but neither could be consoled.

"I went back to Chicago, Emma to Jacksonville where she lived with her Navy husband. Daddy never learned to cope. One day he took his hunting rifle out to the orchard and shot himself. The missus sold the land and moved north to be near Emma.

"After Mandy was killed I heard about Seattle, the mountains, the water and clean air. I thought I could get a domestic job but quickly learned rich folk here don't hire on the colored to care for the house and children like they do down south."

"You said you had two boys, what happened to the other one?"

"Another time child, another time." She closed her eyes.

I kissed her on the cheek and whispered, 'Thank you."

I walked away with a pain in my heart and heaviness in my steps. I knew there was so much she hadn't told me, but enough that added to the great respect I had for her.

I noticed a small grocery store and reached into my pocket and felt the five dollars. I always kept it with me, just in case. It was time. I picked out two cans of chicken noodle soup, a small jar of instant coffee, a can of Spam and two candy bars. Then the magic markers and colored pens got my attention like a neon sign on a dark night. I looked at all the colors, then at the food in my shopping basket. The war began. What to feed? My stomach was growling and my creative spirit was famished. The five dollars was not enough to cover my appetite.

I did the math in my head, put back one candy bar and one can of soup reluctantly.

I chose red and yellow pens and received eighty-three cents change. The pens went into my pocket and I felt myself smiling all the way back to Posy's.

"What's in the bag", she asked when I walked in.

"I've been shopping."

"Why?

"We need meat."

She looked in the bag and laughed, "Spam isn't meat."

"It used to be."

"Far out, a candy bar". She screamed.

"It's your birthday present."

"My birthday isn't for two months."

"Gotcha," I smiled.

"That's not fair." There was something in her voice as she backed away, like an animal does when confronted.

Suddenly I saw something moving out the window. A pigeon had landed on the window ledge. "Oh, look," I whispered, sneaking toward the window on my tiptoes.

"What are you doing?"

I opened the window a crack and it didn't move. I got a cracker and slid a piece under the bottom of the window. It began to peck at it.

"Hope, don't feed it, it will never go away."

"So? How much can a pigeon eat? Look how cute it is."

Posy laughed sarcastically.

"Stop it, you're going to hurt his feelings."

"Feelings? Oh please. We can't take on everything that comes along,"

"Oh really? You took me on and what are Auntie Bea and her gang all about? You're full of it Posy. It's a bird. It flies. It's a one shot deal."

Only it wasn't. We didn't realize how long one shot could echo.

He began each day cooing us awake. He became "Malcolm." We couldn't always feed him, but he came and he stayed long enough to touch something in us with his preening and bobbing. His beady red eyes looked at us as though he understood far more than we did. In the protection of the corner of the window ledge he would pull into himself and sleep. He would fly away, perhaps to survey the city and then return again.

Posy's birthday was drawing closer. I thought it strange that her birthday was the same week as my mother's. How do you gift wrap the ghost of birthdays past? I needed a plan, I needed money.

Two blocks down the street I saw the "Help Wanted" sign in the café window. I didn't hesitate a moment.

"Hello, I want to see someone about the job."

"I'm the someone," a tall, slim unsmiling woman behind the cash register said in a gruff voice. "I'm looking for someone to come in at six in the morning to get things ready for the day. It will take two or three hours, the pay is two dollars an hour."

"Hey Trudy, can we get some coffee down here?" a man yelled.

"The pot is right in front of you. Either hold your horses or get it yourself."

"I'm the someone," I smiled. I liked her style.

"Start tomorrow then."

"Perfect. My name is Hope."

"Trudy." She held out her hand. We shook on the deal and she smiled faintly.

I ran down the hill to find Auntie Bea. Breathless and excited I flopped in the lawn chair.

"Land sakes girl, take a breath. What's got you all riled up?"

"I got a job, café down the street, start tomorrow morning at six, just a few hours, Posy's birthday" I was hyperventilating.

"Settle down, breathe."

"O. K. O.K. I'm O.K. Posy is having a birthday soon."

"Posy is having a birthday, how do you know?"

"She told me in a weak moment."

"That's hard to believe."

"Anyway, I want to have a party for her and make her something that will knock her socks off. I will have to make it here though so she won't find it."

"Are you crazy girl? Parties cost money and in case you haven't noticed, not much of that in these parts."

"You're not listening. I got a job and I have it all figured out. Posy won't know because she leaves before I will and I'll be back about the same time. At the day-old bakery store there are cakes with beautiful flowers on them and they are half-price. We can have everyone come and you can give her a song. That would just be the best."

I could see the wheels turning in her head before the twinkle and the smile. She clapped her hands, "O.K. All right. It's a plan. I'll send out the word."

She gave me a big hug and I ran down the street full of lovely details dancing in my head.

The next morning I woke up with a promise to keep and a goal to reach. I jumped in the tub, washed my hair and put on my best jeans and T-shirt. I gave Malcolm an orange rind and cracker. He was broadening his culinary repertoire.

"You, Mister, are the icing on the cake," I smiled. He

rubbed my hand with his head, leaving a soft glow on my fingers.

I was early and Trudy seemed pleased when she unlocked the front door to let me in. She showed me what she wanted me to do. I filled the sugar containers, napkin holders, salt and pepper shakers. The counter top, tables, floors and bathrooms were scrubbed to a shine. I peeled the potatoes and put them in the big tub of cold water, ready for the day's French fries.

It seemed like only a moment had passed when she said, "Have a seat, I'll make you some breakfast."

I felt guilty eating the scrambled eggs and toast. Posy wouldn't have a hot breakfast. Everyday after I finished my work, Trudy would fix me something to eat and we would chat over hot coffee. I liked her; she didn't seem like a boss.

The job gave me purpose. I felt a part of something and I had a goal to work toward. Posy's birthday was like planning a secret mission. One day I saw a big brown shopping bag in the storeroom. It had rope handles on it, the very kind I needed for my project. Trudy was kind enough to give it to me.

In spite of the excitement there were moments when memories of my family came out of the shadows to hound me. The numbers on the calendar on the café wall also counted down to my mother's birthday like the long slow pendulum of the clock that belonged to my Grandma.

My older sister and I had loved her birthday and we worked for weeks on macaroni necklaces, drawings, and paper mâché forms we called Creatures.

"Oh you girls, you shouldn't have gone to such a fuss,"

she would giggle as she opened her gifts wrapped in brown paper and tied with red yarn. She saved each and every gift in a box she called her treasure box.

It was always a toss-up as to what direction special days would take. If my father came home, or if he didn't, either way he ruined it. He could make things right if he came home sober and brought flowers, but that never happened. His good intentions were buried under his own selfish excuses.

"Hope, honey are you alright?" Trudy was patting my back.

"What? Oh, I'm sorry. Yeah, I'm fine." I wiped my tears with my sleeve.

"Sit down," Trudy's voice was kind and firm.

"I'm fine. I have work to do."

"I said sit down. The last time I checked, I'm still your boss. I've seen that look a few times; it's a homesick look. Do you want to talk?"

"No"

"OK. Fine, if you don't want to talk to me, go call your mama." She put a hand full of quarters on the counter and went back into the kitchen

I didn't know what to do. Then I thought of mom and what she must be thinking as her birthday was coming and how worried she must be. I picked up the coins, took a deep breath, put them in the slots on the phone, dialed the number and listened to the ring.

"Hello."

"Hi mom, it's me. Happy Birthday early. I don't want

to talk, just wanted you to know I'm fine and that I love you very much. It wasn't you mom, it was never you. Good bye." I could hear her yelling my name as I hung up the phone. I stood unable to move, feeling for the first time how far away she was. I could see her in the kitchen holding the dead receiver in her hand.

The next afternoon I took the bag and pens to show Auntie Bea.

"What are you going to do with that bag?" She asked.

"Make magic."

She leaned over and watched intently while I began to draw flowers on the sides of the bag. I colored them with the pens.

"I need green for the leaves, I don't have green."

"Get green, and purple too. My my, that's pretty."

"It's to go with Posy's hat. She will have a designer bag to carry her stuff in."

"You're good, you know. Some kind of fancy artist you are."

"Am I an artist, Auntie Bea?"

"You tell me."

"I don't know, I just like to draw things."

"That's a good start," She smiled.

"I have to go now, please hide this so no one sees it. I'll get more pens when I get paid and finish it."

I gave her a big hug and went back to Posy's.

I was feeding Malcolm when she came through the door so quietly she scared me. She was ashen faced and stooped like an old woman.

"What?" I asked.

She began to shake all over. I was frightened.

"We have been sold out," She whimpered.

"What? What do you mean?"

"Our building is being demolished, blown up, bang, bye bye."

"What are you talking about?" I felt faint. My voice sounded like it was coming from a tunnel.

"They are building condos."

"They who? They can't do that."

"Listen Hope. THEY can do anything THEY want. When developers cut down the forest, does the squirrel get to vote?"

"We can find something else somewhere."

"You don't get it. I make a hundred and fifty lousy dollars a month, seventy-five of that goes to rent because it's a favor. Most of what's left over I save because I'm flushing this toilet someday. This is not my last bus stop. So what do you want to do with your life.?"

I opened my backpack and handed her my sketchbook. "That's what I want to do with the rest of my life. Don't look at it now. I need some air, I'm going for a walk."

I walked in a daze, unable to think through the spinning in my head. I wandered until I saw a corner that had grass, some trees and a few benches. Someone was calling my name, "Hope, Hope." Suddenly my eyes focused and from the blur I saw Auntie Bea sitting on one of the benches.

I ran to her and fell into her arms sobbing. "They are going to destroy our building."

"I heard. Look at me child. A building is like a heart. Without love and care it can sour and rot. Sometimes the damage is so bad it needs more than anything can be done." She held me until I cried myself limp.

"Posy told me. I think she's scared and I didn't tell her about my job. It will ruin the surprise."

"It doesn't have to. You should tell her, it might take some of the fear away. That is if you plan on staying around. She doesn't have to know about her birthday party."

She began to cough. It was a shallow hacking at first, then almost a dry wretch. She took deep panting breaths and the coughing subsided. "Nothing to worry about, it comes and goes."

I was frightened. "Are you sure?"

"I'm sure."

We sat in silence watching the birds play tag on the grass. I didn't want to leave her and I was worried about Posy. I felt like a wishbone, ready to split in half.

She took my hand, "You go on now. Just remember that life is just moments piled on top of each other and you get through it one at a time. You girls stick together and everything will be fine."

Posy was looking out the window when I walked in the door. She didn't turn around.

"Where did you hear about this?"

"It's buzzing all over the streets." She turned and looked

me hard in the eye; "I love your drawings by the way."

"Thanks, I have something to tell you. I have a job at the café down the street. I go in at six in the morning and work until around eight. It isn't much, but better than nothing and I think it might work into something better. I have only been there a week and I was saving the news as a surprise for later. So, that means I can contribute, I don't take advantage of people."

There was a knock at the door before she could respond. I opened the door and the landlord was standing there. "Can I come in?"

He stood in the middle of the room. Posy turned and was all over him before he could open his mouth.

"What do you think you're doing? How can you sell people's home right out from under them? You slimy turncoat. I just want to beat the crap out of you."

He watched Posy's skinny frame raging toward him, "Posy, settle down." He tried not to laugh.

"Settle down? What audacity. That's easy for you to say. We lose our home and all your problems go up in dust. You walk away with a fat wad of money in your wallet. Settle down? You ain't seen nothin yet, I'm just getting warmed up."

I had to give him credit; he just stood there taking the punches.

Finally he shouted at her, "Shut up and listen to reason for a change."

She stepped back away from him and didn't say another word.

"Look, there was a code inspection. This building failed on too many counts. There is no way I could fix everything that is wrong. Mr. Thornson contacted me. He has wanted to buy the property for a long time. This is prime real estate as far as the land goes. The building is worthless. I had no choice, I had to sell. I'm sorry. It won't be until spring sometime so there is time. I want to be fair. You have always paid on time; I can't say that about everybody. This is what I want. How about I waive the rent from now till then? Gives you a chance to sock away a bit. I got a down payment, so I have no problem with that."

"That's nice of you, but how do we stop this all together?" Posy wasn't going down easily.

He shook his head; "You can't fight City Hall."

"Want to bet. You can always fight, winning is the question."

He opened the door, turned to look at Posy as if to say something, changed his mind and became a shadow going down the hall. Posy fell on the bed and screamed into a pillow.

"How do we fight City Hall?" I asked.

"First we find it."

The next morning we dressed in the best clothes we had. Posy reached for her hat, as we were about to walk out the door.

"Posy, no offense, but you can't wear that, no one will take us seriously."

"A lady wears a hat to town."

"We have to blend in, and act confidant or we will get nowhere fast."

"Oh, alright!"

Once on the street we got directions from someone wearing a suit and carrying a briefcase. We scaled the hills to Fourth Street and caught a bus south to City Hall.

Inside, in the lobby, people were everywhere. Some were dressed in business suits; others were the common folks. They all had a mission of some kind.

We read the Directory, found the elevators and tried to get into one, but they were all full. At last, we elbowed our way in and Posy pushed the button to our floor.

We walked into the City Clerks office, heads high and smiling. We felt like we were about to slay the dragon

"Excuse me." Posy said to the lady behind the desk.

"May I help you?"

"Yes you can. We want to talk to the Mayor."

"He isn't in this office."

"So what office would he be in?"

"Why do you want to talk to the Mayor?" As if telling her would make all the difference in the world.

Posy was becoming frustrated. "Because he is in charge of the city, we believe in going to the top. This is a city issue. Some developer is blowing up our building and is going to put up condos. We want to stop it."

"I see. I suggest you go to the planing department, down the hall to the left." She tried everything to squelch a grin.

We walked in the door marked Planning Department.

"May I help you?" The very stern lady asked.

"Well, yes you can as a matter of fact. We want to talk to the Mayor." Posy gave her a big smile.

"Excuse me?"

"The Mayor, we need to see him."

"You're in the wrong department."

"No we aren't. The lady in the City Clerks office sent us here."

"Why?"

"Because we were in the wrong department." Posy said emphatically.

"Look, we have a problem." As I explained the situation to her I could see her soften. She listened and didn't interrupt me.

"I fully understand how you feel but there are several considerations here. First of all that area was built before codes were not as strict as they are now; before we knew about earthquakes and all that stuff. If the owner of the building didn't maintain the building to meet the new codes, we have to consider that a violation. Second of all, he has a right to sell. Also, if the developer is going to rebuild on the property, he has to have all his permits in order. It sounds to me like everything is legal and there isn't anything that can be done, I'm sorry."

"Can't the Mayor do anything?"

"No, the owner and developer are within the law."

"Thank you for your time." Posy was trying not to cry.

Defeated, we left the building and stood on the sidewalk without talking. We got on the bus and went back to our neighborhood where we felt we were living with a lit fuse.

We tried to carry on as usual. I chose to shove it away far enough to give me room to breathe. Posy shifted from gloom to not dealing with it at all.

I moved forward with birthday plans. Auntie Bea worked on her end and I worked on mine. We decided to have the party a month early to make it a real surprise and to have something to lighten our spirits. Trudy offered to make a roasted chicken dinner with all the trimmings. I bought a cake at the day-old store and left it with Auntie Bea. I bought Posy some socks, batteries for her radio and a book about flowers. I put them in her bag and covered them with tissue paper.

We were ready. Everyone had their game plan. Posy was playing Solitaire with Flash's cards and I was getting more nervous with every shuffle.

There was a knock at the door. Finally! I opened the door and winked at Flash.

He came in and gave Posy a story that someone had stolen the bike from the guy that loaned it to her, and that he wanted to talk to her.

"That's great, just what I need right now. Where is he?"

"Down on the corner."

As soon as they left people filed in like a Military Drill Team. Trudy had everything in carry-out boxes with paper plates and silverware. Auntie Bea had the bag and the cake. Everyone took a place on the floor.

We could hear Posy in the hall, obviously annoyed, "Come on Flash, you said he was down on the corner, where is he?"

"How do I know?"

They opened the door and we all yelled, "Surprise,"

Posy just stood there looking around the room. She started crying and bolted out the door with Flash right behind her. I wondered if I had made a mistake.

"It will be just fine," Auntie Bea said.

At last Posy opened the door and Flash pushed her inside. I gave her a hug and she started crying again. "I don't know what to do."

"Be Queen For a Day."

"Sure, like I know how to do that."

"Come, sit by me child." Auntie Bea motioned.

I went into the bathroom and wet a washcloth and handed it to her. "Wipe your snotty nose and put on your hat."

"Yeah, that's better." She looked at Trudy from under the brim; "Do I know you?"

"I'm Trudy, Hope's boss and friend,"

"Nice to meet you."

I handed her the bag and she turned it around looking at both sides, "This is so beautiful, it goes with my hat."

"That's the whole point, it needs more work on it though."

"It's beauty in process." She struggled not to cry again.

We ate until we could hardly move. Auntie Bea sang with Flash and others joined in while Jake played the harmonica.

When they left, there seemed to be a hole in the room, it was empty and quiet. We didn't talk for a long time.

"People really love you Posy," I said at last.

"It's the hardest thing I have ever had to deal with," she touched the bag tenderly like she stroked Malcolm's back.

I fell asleep that night full of more joy than I could remember.

The hot days were turning short and cooler. The low light of autumn was deceiving, playing games with the clock. The sun gave the false impression that summer was endless. People knowing otherwise hung on to every day of warmth, dreading the inevitable.

A forbidding gloom set over the city, in various shades of gray. The horizon line across the Sound vanished. The Olympic Mountains, which were once sparkling spikes became a murky, blurred outline. The rain could be a soft mist or a pounding splashing monster.

We taped a piece of cardboard to the inside of the window ledge and Malcolm had learned to trust us enough to come inside on the cardboard to eat and preen his wet feathers.

I took a change of clothes to the café so I would have something dry to wear. Posy covered herself in plastic trash bags to go to the Market for the flimsy produce left from the abundant harvest. Her newspapers were distributed in plastic sleeves.

We were dry, but not always warm. The chill seeped through the walls and the small heater was not competent to overtake the power of the cold. Life under the bridge, however, was soggy and lethargic. The residents huddled together under plastic tarp tents. The robust summer singing became a soft hum or only silence. Some gave in and went to shelters. Others moved on. Auntie Bea, Flash, and the close-knit stayed together and dug in for the long haul.

Sometimes they would come and share our roof and hot soup. Auntie Bea always protested, not wanting to impose. We played cards and they were able to sleep a dry slumber.

It came without warning in the night. A white phantom blew across the city, paralyzing everything in its path. I awoke to a mysterious silence, a heavy stillness. The familiar morning noises, taken for granted, were gone. I crawled out of bed and was assaulted by the cold. I put on another sweater and went to the window. Malcolm was waiting, huddled down and covered with snow. I forced the window open, picked him up and put him under my first sweater. He rustled, trying to get closer to me.

I looked down at the street below. Nothing was moving. The cars parked along the street were big white puffs. Huge flakes continued to float to the ground.

"Posy, get up, hurry. We have a problem. It's been snowing big time, looks like all night." She was out of bed, throwing on anything in sight while I gave Malcolm a cracker.

We ran down the stairs and out into the white. We ignored the cold and the fact that we only wore tennis shoes and light jackets over our sweaters. It was impossible to run in the snow that came up almost to our knees.

Traffic, as light as it was, skidded sideways trying to avoid crashing into each other. Posy ran into the street. The sound of horns pierced the chill. She waved her arms screaming at the cars that couldn't stop. "Slow down, I have to get over there."

I couldn't watch any longer, I lifted my feet and plodded forward, dodging a cab I joined her in the middle of the street. When there was an opportunity we pounded our way to the other side.

Under the bridge, people were standing close together in a circle bending over Auntie Bea's chair.

"Let me in." Posy was screaming and pushing her way through.

Flash was on the ground rocking Auntie Bea gently in his arms. Her face was ashen and dotted with perspiration. She was shivering under the afghan that had been put over her. She smiled faintly at us as we knelt beside her.

She whispered so softly that we had to bend close to her to hear her say, "There is an envelope in that box under my chair."

Posy found the old shoebox and put it beside her. She motioned to Flash and pointed to the box. "Your ticket out of hell, son." And she was gone.

Flash threw his head back and snow fell on his face. "Mama," he screamed at the sky like a wolf howling for a lost mate. He continued to rock her back and forth and pulled the old afghan up under her neck.

I knelt down beside him and put my arms around him, "I didn't know she was your mother," I whispered.

"No one did, that's the way she wanted it." He began to tremble in my arms, unable to control his sobbing.

I turned to look for Posy but she was gone. I wanted to

find her but I couldn't move. In a moment she was back, "I called someone" was all she said.

Flash struggle to his feet, ran his sleeve across his face and picked up the box. He untied the heavy red yarn around the box and slowly removed the lid. Inside, a musty smell, a crisp sunflower and an old photo of a family. The father in bib overalls, looking stern and proud. The mother, small but strong with the unfinished afghan across her lap. Sitting on the ground beside the mother, a little girl in pigtails and holding a rag doll with button eyes. The child looked shyly into the camera.

Flash tenderly touched the little girl's face. He leafed through the box and pulled out a photograph of a young man in uniform, a pair of dog tags on a chain and the small box that held The Purple Heart. There were letters tied together with string. At the bottom of the box was a large ragged yellow envelope. When he opened it, money scattered all over the ground, fives, tens, twenty's and a few hundreds. Not one person moved to touch it, they just stood there looking. Flash was on his hands and knees picking up the bills and stuffing them into his pockets.

He went over to his mother, bent down and moaned, "All this time you were hoarding this, and all this time you were going without and praising Jesus. We have been hungry, not ready-for-supper-hungry but gut-pain-hungry. Was it worth it mama, was it?" He fell to his knees and took her in his arms again.

The white ambulance came. Reluctantly Flash let go of

her. Gently, they put her on a stretcher. As they were sliding her into the ambulance the afghan fell at my feet. "Take it," Flash said. "She just gave it to you."

I picked it up and cried into it like I had cried into her bosom so many times. Before they closed the door, Posy kissed her cheek and bowed her head.

A police car had come with the ambulance but had parked a respectable distance away. Flash went over to the policeman and they talked awhile. Then Flash got into the passenger side of the police car and they drove away behind the ambulance.

That was the moment the world stopped. We all just stood there. Then Jake spoke up, "We need to have some kind of memorial service or something, it can't just end like this."

"In three days maybe when the snow melts," Posy said.

Jake thought that would be a good time, "I'll tell Flash."

Thanks to a warm southwest breeze, the snow melted almost as fast as it had come. Two days later there was a knock on the door. It was Flash. "Can you come now?"

"Sure," Posy said. She picked up her hat and we followed Flash down the stares. I wondered why she wanted the hat, but didn't ask.

When we reached the street, Flash turned and said, "I took some of mama's money and had her buried proper. I wasn't going to put her in a potter's field."

We joined the others beside Auntie Bea's chair.

"I just want to say a few words regarding my mama. She was a good woman, she loved God with all her heart, she loved me, and she loved you. She never thought about herself, only as far as how could she maintain herself to be able to help someone else. She is probably directing God's choir right now. I only hope I can live the rest of my life to make her proud." Flash bowed his head.

After a few moments he raised his head and in his most powerful baritone voice sang the words, "Amazing Grace", then he stopped. Then everyone sang the words, "That saved a wretch like me", and then they stopped. They sang, "I once was lost" and stopped, and sang, "was blind' and stopped. I realized that the silent parts were where Auntie Bea would sing. Remembering her voice, I could hear her fill in the spaces.

When the song was finished with, "and grace will lead me home" Posy took her hat over to Auntie Bea's chair. She began taking the flowers off the hat, one at a time and laying them in the chair. When all that was left of the hat was naked straw, she put it on the ground at the foot of the chair and said through her tears, "This was her pulpit after all."

We walked away knowing nothing would ever be the same. Nothing would ever fill the hole that she left.

We were like robots that winter, moving through the days on command. I was working at the café full time waiting tables. Trudy let us eat there once a day for free. I made good tips and the pay was decent.

We lived close to the bone and saved as much money as we could. We were reminded of Auntie Bea when we put change and bills in the coffee can.

We never saw Flash again. We heard he might be at the Gospel Mission, but didn't know for sure. We figured if he had wanted to see us he would come by, but he never did.

We plodded through one ugly gray day after another. Our joy had been snatched away from us.

PART TWO

The days became longer and brighter. The rain was more intermediate and less relentless.

And, as if there were no water left in the sky, the clouds split, exposing the blue that had been only a memory for so long. The sun was a Pied Piper, bringing the city out of hibernation and drying out soggy spirits. Flowers in hanging baskets on the light posts began to bloom almost overnight. The Olympic Mountains rose out of the Sound, dazzling with winter snow. Mount Rainier shot up behind the city skyline like it grew in the valley when our backs were turned. Umbrellas and yellow slickers were traded for bare chests and sunglasses. There was a slow frenzy as bicycles and roller-skates emerged out of the dark places where they had hibernated all winter.

Once again the waterfront came to life after a long sleep. Fish Kites, shaped like fish played tag with seagulls in the sky.

At last there was music; full volume speakers blasted from open car windows, guitar players again on the street and birds had found their voice. This was bittersweet for Posy and me.

We missed Auntie Bea. I could hear her sweet voice in my head and my heart longed to talk with her just one more time. Posy didn't go to the market for produce anymore, there was no one left to receive it.

Pioneer Square opened its arms to tourists and locals weaving in and out of high-end shops and art galleries. Humanity began to shed its winter skin.

Even though we were thawing, the dooms-day chill hung in the air. Spring brought borrowed time for adjustment. We began to look for options but so far had hit a brick wall at every turn. The demolition had been delayed twice. Somehow we hoped it wouldn't happen at all.

One day, to give us a respite from focusing on survival mode, we went to Pioneer Square. We pretended we were from out of town, pretended we were rich and "dressing down." We walked slowly, taking in the sights like we had never seen them before. We ate an ice-cream cone, and for once felt that we fit in.

Outside a gallery Posy pressed her nose to the window. "Have you ever seen anything like it?"

I couldn't speak. The painting was huge, hugged by a wide hand-carved gold-leaf frame. Titled "The Grand Canyon at Sunset", it drew me into it like a magnet. I was smitten breathless by the colors and the way the light kissed the tops of the red rocks.

We stood at the window in silence, taking in the magnificence of the painting, Posy stepped backwards to get a wider view and I heard a crunching sound behind me. A well-dressed woman in a business suit came tearing out of the gallery just as Posy stepped backwards and they collided.

The woman was shaken as she looked at Posy sitting on the sidewalk, "I'm so sorry. Are you alright?"

Posy, on the other hand, was not feeling her remorse. "What were you doing? Not watching where you were going, that's for sure."

She began picking up her stuff that was scattered all over the sidewalk, putting it back into her bag. The woman was on her hands and knees trying to help.

"I'll get it myself," Posy sneered at her.

The woman wasn't moved by the sarcasm. "What a beautiful bag," she said. "Where did you get it?"

Posy pointed to me; "She made it. She's a fantastic artist."

What had been hostility had changed to chumminess. They were sitting in the middle of the sidewalk having a meeting, oblivious to the passers-by walking around them.

The woman got to her feet, pulled her skirt down, rearranged her jacket, and checked her nylons for tares or runs.

Still looking at Posy's bag in her hand she said, "I want one of these. No, wait, I want to borrow this for five minutes. Don't go anywhere, I'll be right back, trust me."

She vanished behind the Grand Canyon leaving us standing there shell-shocked.

"What was that?" I mumbled.

"I don't know. We'll have to wait and see."

The woman returned later rather than sooner, carrying

the bag and a big smile, "Come with me. The gallery wants to buy some and I want one for myself."

A voice that sounded like mine said, "You can't be serious."

"My lunch hour ended twenty minutes ago and I'm still here. I'm very serious." She was stolidly insistent.

"Who are you?" I was puzzled.

"A Mack truck that knows talent when I see it," she laughed.

We followed her into the gallery with no idea what to expect. The light was low with track lights that shone on the paintings. There was thick carpet on the floors. Pedestals held statues or blown glass vases. In the middle of the room was a large circular couch surrounding a glass coffee table. Soft music was playing. The glass display case held beautiful gift items. I took it all in. It was so grand I wanted to cry. I had never been in a real art gallery before.

A tall slim man with a friendly smile approached us. "Veronica darling, is this the artist you told me about?"

"I'm the artist's manager," Posy said.

"Yes, I'll bet you are. Let me see your bag again."

Posy handed it to him and said, "It's one of a kind, no two are alike."

For a moment I thought I had slipped into a coma and was dreaming. What was this 'no two' business?

"Fabulous!' He said. "How many of these can I have?"

"What?" was all I could say.

"How many can I get and how much are they wholesale?"

What's wholesale I thought, but not wanting to look as stupid as I felt, I said, "I can do ten for you for twenty dollars each, half in advance for supplies, and two weeks work time."

"Fine. Your name is?"

"My name is Hope, this is Posy."

"Nice to meet you, both of you," he smiled and handed me five twenty dollar bills.

"Trust me, you won't be sorry," I said.

"I don't know why I should, but I do.'"

"Thank you, I'll see you in two weeks."

Out on the sidewalk, Veronica looked at her gold watch. "I am so late, I'll meet you here in two weeks, at noon. I'll pay you for my bag then. Nice running into you," She winked at Posy and started sprinting down the street.

"What just happened here?"

"I don't know, but don't ask me to take a fall for you again." We both laughed.

Veronica ran into the offices of B.T. Development, breathless and disheveled. She looked at her watch, "Where is he?" she panted to the receptionist.

"In his office."

"Does he know I'm late?"

"No, he only asked for you once."

"Great, I'm going in."

She opened the hand carved mahogany door and stepped into

the plush room that was more like a den than an office. He sat on a large leather couch with papers strung out on a coffee table. He had a desk under the floor-to-ceiling windows, but he liked the freedom of organized chaos.

"Burke?" Veronica addressed him with cautious familiarity. He didn't look up, but continued to write and gestured toward the windows with his left hand.

"Is that sunshine out there? How was lunch? The City Planning Department is giving me fits. I need you to take them a packet and give them a reality check."

"Burke?"

"What?" He looked up at her and was shocked at what he saw. The always perfectly groomed assistant stood before him in complete disarray; torn stockings, hair going in different directions and eyes far too wide for her delicate face.

"What did you have for lunch?"

"This isn't a good time to talk to you, you obviously have too much on your mind." She was still breathless.

"Give me an hour, I should have this together by then, in the mean time you might get yourself together."

She left him with his papers and went into the lady's room. When she looked in the mirror she laughed in spite of her embarrassment.

She combed her hair, picked up her messages and went to her office. She found the new nylons in her desk drawer and put them on. For a few moments she sat looking out the window trying to relax, then started returning phone calls.

Soon, the intercom buzzed, "Burke can see you now."

She walked into his office and watched him looking out the window, knowing that's what he did when he had too much on his mind. He turned around and looked at her.

"Everybody is dragging their feet on issuing permits. My crew is sitting on their butts waiting, and we can't move forward. If I don't get moving on that property, we get closer to having to go into winter, then beaucoup bucks are just thrown away for nothing. So, you wanted to talk to me? What's up? You look better, by the way. What hit you on your lunch hour?"

"A pint-size whirlwind. I went to the gallery and ran into two girls, literally, I ran into one of them. Anyway, I discovered that one of them is a raw artistic talent, the other one has the mouth and attitude of a corporate executive."

"And this should interest me how?"

"They are out there waiting to set the world on fire, they just don't know it yet. They are an investment waiting to happen,"

"NO. No way, not a chance. Don't be bringing me your stray kittens. I thought you had a job."

"I do. You are my job and my job is to help you make money. When I see talent in one hand and money in the other hand, I want to clap."

"Yea, well, my hands are too busy juggling."

"Fine, but while your balls are in the air, you might keep an open mind."

"What do you want from me?"

"I don't know yet."

She told him about the bags and how the gallery had ordered ten on the spot and had paid half in advance.

61

"O.K. Look, I ordered a bag for myself, I pick it up two weeks from today. When I show it to you, be prepared to be dazzled."

"I don't get dazzled."

"There is a first time for everything. I have to get back to work." She knew she had hit a brick wall and over-talking was not going to get her anywhere. She would wait until she had the bag in hand and it would speak for itself.

I sat on the floor surrounded by bags, colored pens and confusion. Trudy had found a place that sold bags wholesale and gave them to me. 'I want to invest in a sure thing,' she had said. I had taken thirty dollars of the money the gallery had given me and bought every color of pen I needed, then put seventy dollars in the coffee can.

I was stocked and ready to go but was afraid to begin, afraid I might make a mistake and ruin a bag. First, I put red tape around the seams of all of the bags. Now I was committed. Intimidated and overwhelmed I drew a small flower in the bottom corner of one of the bags, then added to it with leaves, then another flower, and then a butterfly. Before I knew it, the first bag was finished and I had begun the next, moving around the sides, up and down, losing track of anything else. I walked into the garden on the brown paper. I remembered when my mother bought jumbo boxes of crayons and a pile of coloring books for me. My child's hand would do its best to stay in the lines as I watched the color go down on the page with Mickey Mouse or Donald Duck.

I put down the pen, got up and walked around the bags. I

had never had so much of my work to see all at once. I looked up and saw Posy standing in the door.

"Those are bloomin beautiful," she smiled.

"Really?"

"Really. How are you going to sign them?"

"I don't know, I haven't thought about signing them."

"You have to."

I thought a moment. "I've got it. Remember when we first met and you said your hat was a garden? Then I made the bag to go with your hat."

I took a black pen and wrote 'Hope's Garden' in small letters at the bottom of one of the bags.

"That's it. Fantastic!" Posy squealed clapping her hands.

I worked on the bags in the evening when I finished working at the café. I finished them two days early. They were all lined up against the wall. Now I had to look at them and wait. I was torturing myself. What if the guy at the gallery hated them, then what? What if the lady didn't show up. I spun out of control inside of my head. I looked at the bags, over and over and saw all the things I could have done better. I felt like I was trapped in a cage with no way out.

Delivery day came far too soon. I folded the bags, stacked one on top of another and tied them with red ribbon. I dressed and waited as the clock ticked down to the moment of my fate. Posy ran a comb through her hair and we were out the door.

We stood in front of the gallery, we were a half an hour early. I was paralyzed with fear.

"Posy, you take them in, I don't want to go in there."

"No way. It's your work and you have to face the music regardless of the song. Don't make me drag you in there. What kind of impression would that make? Take a deep breath and smile whether you feel like it or not. Come on, it's show time."

He greeted us with an aloof smile, which I didn't take as a good sign. I randomly set aside one bag for the lady. I couldn't remember her name. He untied the ribbon, spread the bags out on the counter and looked at each one without comment. The silence was killing me. I couldn't read anything from his stoic face. It seemed like hours before he spoke, "Fantastic!" He then put three in a glass display case where they could be seen from both sides. I was speechless and close to tears. I didn't know how to be professionally blasé.

He paid me in cash, counting out the bills as he put them in my shaking hand, "I'm going to need your Social Security number down the road. I need to pay in checks so I can keep my records straight." Now he was smiling.

When I turned around I saw the lady standing there with a big grin. I handed her the bag. She looked at it from all angles, "I love it, I just love it. Here's my card. I want you to call me in a couple of weeks."

"Why?"

"Just call. Trust me." And she walked out the door.

I thanked the gallery man and we left. In front of the Grand Canyon again I put the card in my pocket. I shook my head, "It just gets weirder by the moment."

I looked at the money. The lady had given me two tens, and the gallery had given me five twenties. I put the twenties and one ten in my pocket and held the other ten over my head, "This is lunch money. Let's find the biggest cheeseburgers on the planet."

"Yo, Mama," Posy screamed.

Veronica was at her desk when Burke walked in carrying a briefcase in each hand. "What's that stupid grin about?" *He asked.*

"In a moment. How's the project going?"

"Slow, frustrating."

"How's your mood?"

"Like it always is."

"Charming, right?"

"Absolutely charming."

"Great, can I talk to you then?"

"Are we back to that again?"

"Yes, we are."

"I don't have a lot of time."

"Whatever." She took the bag from under her desk and followed him into his office. She sat it on the coffee table. She watched his mood change when he picked it up and looked carefully at both sides.

"Wow," he said.

"Did I hear you say, 'Wow?'"

"Hope's Garden. Very clever. I like the colors and the free almost childlike style. However, I don't have time for anything

more in my life. Did you say the gallery ordered these? How did it go?" He turned the bag around several times and put it back on the coffee table.

"He ordered ten. She delivered on time, he loved them and paid her twenty bucks each, wholesale."

"I feel an "and" coming on." He put his arms over his head as if to protect himself from falling debris.

"I told them to call me in a couple of weeks, I gave them my card."

"Oh, man. Did you commit me to anything? I don't even know what I'm supposed to do with this."

"I didn't commit you to anything. I didn't even mention your name. If nothing else, I'll buy some for Christmas presents. I don't know what you are to do with this either. Run it around in your head, if you want to meet with them, let me know so I will know what to say if they call."

Posy had started working for a jewelry vendor at the market after she delivered her papers. She received small pay and a commission on what she sold. The only time we saw each other was in the evening. We both worked on Saturdays.

One night she suggested that we empty the coffee can and see how much money we had collected.

"Seems like that rainy day we are saving for is about to hit the fan," she said.

We turned the can upside down on the bed and watched the bills come out. Posy had put the seventy-five dollars that would have gone toward rent into the can and I had put my wages in. I kept the tips separate.

We started counting the bills and when we had them neatly stacked we had over two thousand dollars.

She lifted the corner of the mattress and pulled out a small, bulging brown paper bag. "This is my savings."

I reached into my backpack and retrieved an envelope, "And this is my savings."

"It looks to me that with our coffee can stash we are going to be able to find another place to live if we can find something within reason. I have a thought. If we each put the same amount in the can each month we will have enough to survive. Your savings are yours and mine is mine. Whatever we don't put in the can, we keep separate. Mine is mine, yours is yours. How does that sound?" she asked.

"Sounds fair to me. Even-steven on expenses, independence on what's left over."

"Exactly, that way no one gets their feelings hurt or feels obligated to the other."

"David, at the gallery, said he had to start paying me with a check if the bags sell. Looks like I need to open a bank account if that happens. He also said he needed to keep a record of what he pays, so it would be good for us to put the expense money in the bank and write checks for rent and other stuff."

"Have we now become part of the human race?" She frowned.

"I'm afraid so."

A few days later I realized it was time to call Veronica. I

took her card to work with me. After the lunch crowd was gone I asked Trudy if I could use the phone.

I punched in the number and heard someone say, "B.T. Development, how may I direct your call?"

"Veronica, please."

"Thank you, one moment please."

"Hello, this is Veronica speaking."

"Hi Veronica, this is Hope. You wanted me to call."

"Yes, Hope, it's good to hear from you. I have spoken with my boss about you and he would like to meet you and your friend. Could you come in late tomorrow afternoon around five o'clock? Take a cab, we will reimburse you."

"That will be fine, I'll see you tomorrow."

I hung up the phone and looked at Trudy. I was confused and apprehensive.

"What's up?" She asked

"I'm not sure, but I need to get off early tomorrow if that is o.k. There is a guy that wants to meet me and I have to go."

"Sure, that will be fine."

I ran back to the room full speed that afternoon and fell in the door.

"What?" Posy asked.

I tried to catch my breath. I told her about the phone call and asked if she could go with me.

"Why does this guy want to meet us?"

"I don't know, but we need to go find out."

"Sure, I'll go."

The next day we settled into the backseat of the cab and gave the driver the address. He drove up the hills to the high-rise buildings. He pulled up to a tall gray glass building.

Inside we found the suite number on the directory and stepped into the elevator. We didn't talk. The elevator door opened and the suite was right in front of us across the marble floor of the hall. We stood outside the glass door with gold lettering on it. We took a deep breath and walked into the reception area.

The walls were beautiful polished wood. The carpet was so thick it was difficult to walk on, like trying to balance on Jell-O.

Veronica appeared "Hi. Welcome. Can I get you coffee or something to drink?"

"No thank you," I answered.

We followed her into a lush room. Veronica smiled at the strikingly handsome man on the couch. He stood up when she introduced us.

"Please, have a seat," he said, sitting down.

We sat down on the couch opposite him.

"So, I hear from Veronica that someone is quite an artist." He smiled, looking at both of us.

"That would be her." Posy looked at me.

"Why are we here exactly?"

"I might have a business opportunity for you."

"Which you?" Posy asked.

He shot a glance at Veronica and smiled, "You both."

"What might that be?" Posy was now sitting upright leaning toward him. I watched them both, a bit detached from the whole scene. Veronica brought coffee and put a plate of cookies on the coffee table.

"I'm a business man. Sometimes I invest in things that give me a good return on my money. I know a good product when I see it."

"What do you have in mind?" I asked, taking a sip of coffee.

"I'm not sure yet, but I know you have a marketable product here. I'm working on a project that has been running behind, but it should straighten out soon. Where can I reach you?"

"I work at Trudy's Café, you can reach me there during the day."

"We'll talk in a few weeks." He stood up. We shook hands, thanked him and Veronica. She gave us the cab money and we left.

The ride back was silent. I just wanted to digest the conversation we had in that beautiful office. I didn't want to get my hopes up.

I looked at Posy looking out the window. "I miss Auntie Bea, what would she say right now?"

"Keep your heart and head aligned, child." That's what she would say.

A week later, the notice came, a piece of paper slipped under the door. We read it; To All Residents, this is to inform you— after that it was a blur. We knew it was coming, but only when it was in writing did it become real. We had one week to "Vacate the Premises."

Two days before eviction day we put our meager possessions in a few boxes and took them to the café. Trudy had cleared out the storeroom, brought in a roll-a-way bed and a few linens, giving us a temporary place to stay.

It was the way I was waking up, half-conscious, but aware of the ache in my stomach; a heavy gnawing that hung on like a starving dog.

Perhaps this is what people on Death Row feel on their last day when there is no appeal left, or on the first day after someone dies, and how a mother feels when it has all been said and done, and a daughter runs away from home.

For a while I laid there, and like so many mornings, listened to the traffic sounds. How can people keep doing their lives? I opened my eyes and looked at the window. Malcolm wasn't there, for the first time he wasn't there. Posy was awake, but not moving. Her breathing was more of a choking sound.

We got up and each took our last bath in the room. For a change, we used all the hot water. It didn't matter anymore.

When we walked out I turned and looked at the room. Ghosts seemed to ooze from the walls. I turned and closed the door.

"Why did you do that?" Posy asked, crying.

"What?"

"Close the door?"

"I don't know."

Down the hall there was only the faint odor of some lingering memory. It smelled like popcorn. 'Comfort food' I thought.

Outside, people were everywhere, standing behind yellow police tape. TV cameras were poised and ready.

As we ducked under the yellow tape, Posy said, "Do they think the circus has come to town?"

We joined the crowd and waited. Someone yelled, 'Five, Four.' The building looked forlorn, the black windows like the eyes of a deer looking into its assassin's heart. The crowd was quiet. Then 'Three, Two, One' The building began to tremble, as if overtaken by pain. Then for a moment, long enough to take a breath and hold it, there was no movement. Suddenly, with one violent tremor, it shook and fell into itself. There was a hole in the skyline. Dust clouds billowed upward, hung for an instant, and then began floating down to cover the fallen debris.

Cheers went up from the crowd there to witness the dramatic event. With a push of a button, all that remained was a pile of bricks and the screams of sickening delight.

People began to move away, going back to their lives. It was over. TV crews packed up equipment and drove away. There would be a few seconds on the evening news tonight and some could say they were there. Tomorrow, for them, it would be just another day forgotten.

We were frozen in the aftermath. "Where will Malcolm land?" Posy whimpered.

I turned and started to walk away, my head down watching my feet make little puffs in the powdery dust. I ran into something. I looked up to see the man wearing a hard hat and goggles who had broken my stride. I started to apologize when I thought he looked familiar. I read the name on his hard hat, 'B.T. Development.' I saw white trucks parked behind the yellow tape with the same name on their sides. I felt like I had been shot.

He didn't have a chance to say anything, he obviously recognized me because he started to smile just as I started beating him on the chest with my fists. My anger, confusion, fear and feeling of betrayal erupted in a rage that overtook every cell in my body. I wanted to kill him.

"There aren't enough slimy, profane, words in the English language to describe what you are. You low-life pig. You murdered our home. Is this what has been keeping you so busy?" I screamed.

His hard hat and goggles had fallen to the ground. I stomped on the goggles and kicked the hard hat like a soccer ball. He didn't look nearly as dapper as he had in his fancy office.

He started swatting at me like I was some annoying horse fly. "What's wrong with you, get off me."

"You have the nerve to ask what's wrong with me? You just blew our building to smithereens. There are kids homeless today, thanks to you. I hope this is a good investment for you." I hit him again and kicked him several times on his legs.

He just stood there, making no attempt to defend himself or to strike back. Then the rage was gone. I was limp.

"Have a nice day," I said and started crying. I looked at Posy. She was immobile. Her eyes were huge and her mouth was open, ready to speak, but nothing came out.

"We're out of here," I said, pulling on her arm.

We walked slowly to the café. We sat down in a booth and Trudy brought us iced tea and sat down with us. Her eyes were red from crying.

"I heard the explosion, everything shook. I didn't want to come and see it happen."

Burke limped into the office, pointed to Veronica and said, "Stay away from me. You're evil. I got the stuffing beat out of me by that little lunatic artist friend of yours."

He looked at the receptionist, "Hold each and every call, I don't care who it is. As far as anyone is concerned, I have left the country until further notice. I don't want anyone, and I mean anyone, coming in my office."

He turned, went into his office and slammed the door behind him.

Veronica stood looking at the closed door. She was confused and bewildered. She had never seen him like that. He didn't come out all day and was still in there when she left for home.

He sat on the couch and watched the windows turn grey then dark. He had always prided himself that he was above sentimentalism and maudlin emotions. After all, he cut his teeth on a T-Square and was a builder of steel and concrete.

When he went to work for his father full time he lost his peripheral vision. He kept his focus on the goal, the target of the day.

In the deep recesses of his mind was the dim hope that someday he would go to Africa. Someday he would go to the coast, walk the beach barefooted, or someday he would fall in love, go to church or grow a beard. Now Someday was nipping his Achilles and he was watching the world he had created crumble around him as he looked at the dust from the fallen building that was still on his boots.

He took the pillow from behind his back and pressed into his chest as if trying to plug the gaping bleeding hole somewhere inside of himself.

When the chills came and the shaking rocked him to the core he would sit on the shower floor and listen to the hot water splash on the tile around him.

He found himself praying aloud to the God of his childhood; the one he sang about, 'Jesus loves me this I know.' He wasn't singing now, he was screaming with all of his might, 'WHAT DO YOU WANT FROM ME?' His voice bounced off of one tiled wall to the other and seemed to surround him.

No one screamed back, no one even whispered, but there was a silence that comes only when sound is worn out. He felt like a foreigner in his own life and he didn't understand why.

The next morning she couldn't help herself, she knocked on his door and didn't get an answer.

"Burke, are you in there?"

"Go away," he grumbled.

"Come on, please, let me in."

"Fine, come on in."

He was lying on the couch wearing sweats. His face was unshaven. He didn't look at her.

"You're fired. Everyone's fired."

"Right. Have you been drinking? Did you go home last night?"

"No and no. I mean it, you're fired."

He was bruised and wounded from the inside out. She was looking at a broken man.

"Do you want some coffee?" She asked; not wanting to sound alarmed. She knew she could give him something to salve his open sores but could do nothing to repair the damage to his inner spirit.

"Yes."

She put a carafe of coffee, a glass of water, and a packet of aspirin on the table and sat down on the opposite couch. She didn't talk, waiting for him to take his time.

He looked at her with swollen, blood shot eyes.

"I blew up their home."

"What are you talking about?"

"Your artist and her friend. I blew up their building yesterday. They were there and when it was over Hope turned into a raving maniac, she beat me up and called me names."

"Oh, Burke." She couldn't think of anything else to say.

"You know, I just do what I've always done. It's been about the thrill of tearing things down and building new things. And it's been about the money. I have never been clobbered with the consequences before, never even thought about it." He sighed, got up and looked out the window, his shoulders bent with the weight *of his confusion.*

He turned and looked at her, his face stern, his eyes boring into hers. He came over to the couch, sat down and filled his coffee cup again.

"How long have you worked for me?"

"A little over five years."

"And in five years, how well do you know me? What do I know about you? Who are these people that come and go around here? I hired them, I sign their checks, but who are they, really? What about their families? They show up at the Christmas party with someone, but who is it? What do their kids do? How much money do I have?"

"That's a lot of questions in one fell swoop."

"Yes, and there lies the problem."

"Where are you going with all this?"

"To hell probably. Veronica, I have spent my adult life never seeing beyond blueprints and dollar signs. Buildings never had a face behind them until yesterday when I looked into the eyes of a little wild animal fighting for her life."

"What do you want to do, deep down in your heart?"

"I don't know. Deep down in my heart is not where I go when I need to know what to do."

"That might be a good place to start looking."

"Veronica, do you love anyone?"

"Excuse me?"

"You know, love. Do you honestly love somebody? I've noticed that you never bring anyone to the Christmas party."

"That is none of your business." She got up and opened the

door.

"You have a lot to think about, let me know if you want anything. I can order you lunch if I'm not fired."

He managed a small laugh. "That would be good. I'm just going to hang around here, I don't want to go back to that coffin I refer to as home."

He went into his office bathroom, turned on the shower again and let the steam cloud the mirror. This time he stood under the hot water feeling the pelting on his skin until the water turned cold. He dressed into clean jeans and polo shirt. After he shaved he picked up the phone on his desk and punched Veronica's extension.

"Hi, it's me. I've changed my mind, I'm taking you to lunch. Take the rest of the day off. I need to get some air. Meet me in the parking garage in ten minuets."

"I can't do that, I have work to do."

"So do I. I'm your boss, and you are taking the day off."

"You really have lost your mind. Whatever you say, see you in ten."

"You look better," she said, sliding into the leather seat.

"It's only a façade."

They drove through the city, over the I-90 floating bridge across Lake Washington and east toward the mountains. "Where are we going?" Veronica asked, a bit perplexed.

"Snoqualmie Falls for lunch."

"What have you done with Burke? You look just like him."

He turned on the radio to his favorite station and listened to Booker T and the MG's as the car danced around the curves of Snoqualmie Pass. The blue sky reflected in the river. The air became clear and smelled of hemlock and cedar.

Burke took the exit to Snoqualmie Falls and the adjacent Lodge. They sat by a window in the restaurant and ate crab melts with salad and a glass of wine. They were both taking in the glory of the day and Burke seemed to soften right before her eyes.

After lunch they stood above the falls watching the waters violent descent bouncing off the rocks below. They let the spray settle on their faces.

He turned to look at her, "Who do you love Veronica?"

"I told you, that's none of your business."

They returned to the car and started down the mountain. Burke drove slowly, taking the curves with ease. To Veronica's amazement he began to talk in a most personal way. He told her how he had taken over his father's business after his father suffered a stroke and died shortly afterwards. As the oldest son of three children, it was expected that he would carry out the family name and continue the business. He had gone to college learning architecture and engineering, receiving a degree in both. His father believed in the old school of learning by experience, from the ground up. The only father-son time they shared was when Burke was home from school in the summer and he worked on site with his father.

His mother was a master at not rocking the boat. She understood that her place in the world of the family was as the mute center of the circle. She knew her role was to keep the machine in motion and she played her part with grace. She loved her children from an emotional distance.

He told her that as a little boy he would take his books to bed and become Tom Sawyer, riding the raft of his bed down the river. He went to Africa with Hemingway, propped up his sheets with a yardstick for a mosquito net and listened to the roar of the beasts in the night. He pretended that in Italy he apprenticed for the masters; plastering for frescos, bringing the marble down from the mountain, grinding pigments and watching from the shadows as the great ones created history. He was content in his boyhood dreams to smell the smells and feel the dust.

"And so it is," He sighed.

They returned to the city and Burke pulled into the parking garage of the office building. He parked beside Veronica's car.

"That was a lovely day," she said turning to him.

"Yes it was." He took her head in his hands, leaned toward her and kissed her. She didn't move. When he drew back, ever so slightly, she reached up and touched the graying part of his temples.

He moved away and leaned over the steering wheel. He looked at her again and didn't smile.

"If I sell the business, the house, how long could I survive before I starve to death?"

She laughed, "With your assets, about two hundred years."

He didn't change expression. "You're serious. Are you serious? I'm not sure I want to do this anymore, in fact, I'm not sure I ever wanted to do this at all. I want something else in my life, I want a life."

"Are you having a mid-life crisis?"

"Yes, I am. I'm closing in on mid-life, and I have had a crisis.

I want to do something different. It's me isn't it?"

"Excuse me?" *She knew what was coming.*

"You love me."

She didn't answer him. She reached into her purse for her car keys, wanting to make a quick get-away.

He ignored her attempt to dodge him. "Do you think you can find those girls?"

"Oh, I'm sure you're just the guy they want to see."

"Probably not, but can you try to find them?"

"That's interesting."

"What?"

"Can you try," I'm sort of used to 'just do it."

"Whatever. I'm serious. I want to talk to those kids. How old do you think they are?"

"Probably early to mid-twenties, I would guess. Hope said she worked at Trudy's Café so that might be a good place to look. I wouldn't do it right away though; I would give them some time to kick the dust off their feet. I need to go, I'll see you Monday."

The next morning Veronica opened the drapes in the her front room. The sun came in and caught her in the spot light. She hadn't slept much the night before. She had tried to eat a sandwich but took a couple of bites and threw the rest into the trash. She had gone into the office on Saturday to finish up some work and to clear her desk of papers that had piled up during the week.

Now it was Sunday. She hated Sundays. She wondered what Burke did on Sunday.

It seemed so long ago that she had read the ad in the paper. She had graduated college with a degree in business and was look-

ing for a challenge. The ad had been clear; 'long hours, short pay, room for growth, faint of heart need not apply.' She was hired as his assistant. In three weeks she received a substantial raise.

He had asked her how well she knew him. She thought about that while she made another pot of coffee. Outside of the business, not much. They were a team and the team worked. Within that context, she knew him well. He was driven, high energy, a perfectionist and focused. He had a sense of humor when needed and was a man of great charm.

She looked in the mirror and wondered how the years had piled up on her face so quickly. She wasn't a beauty in the Hollywood sense, but she was striking. Her eyes were far too large for her other features, giving her the look of constant surprise. She smiled at herself and said out loud, "Good morning, Cutie."

She tried to remember when she was first attracted to him. It wasn't a moment, but it came in flashes. It was the way he looked around the room to see if she was in the room at a meeting; it was the strand of hair that fell over his forehead. He could be demanding, impatient and unreasonable, yet he always remembered her birthday. It didn't hurt that he was a gorgeous creature.

"Why did he have to kiss me?" she said out loud. It changed everything. 'I liked loving him from afar,' she thought, throwing herself down on the couch.

The telephone ring sounded like a fire truck siren. She didn't answer it. It didn't stop. After six rings, she couldn't stand it any longer, picking up the receiver she said, "What?"

"Hi, it's me. Can I come over? I need to talk to you."

"No Burke, I'm just lounging around, this isn't a good time.

Anyway you've never come over."

"I just can't go through the day with you in my head and not seeing you."

"Right now I need to be alone with my thoughts and figure them out by myself."

"I appreciate your honesty. A little distance could be a good thing. I'm a little impulsive sometimes, you know. Have a good day Veronica."

"You too. Take care of yourself."

"Bye."

"See ya." With the motion of lying the phone down she knew she had just put the lid on life, as she had known it.

She tried to watch a movie on TV but was too restless. She opened the refrigerator and the light was shocking, almost as much as the dried up green Jell-O.

She took a bath, hoping it would relax her enough to get some sleep. Sleep came in intermediate spurts. Then she was wide-awake pounding on her pillow. There wasn't a spot on the mattress that welcomed her exhausted body.

At the first hint of dawn, she gave up the fight and got up, plugged in the coffeepot and waited for the rich aroma to fill the kitchen.

She stood in her closet staring at the mass of clothes hanging neatly on the padded hangers. What had always been routine now suddenly became a confusing chore. What to wear to work? Low cut or high neck? Skirt or slacks? Bare it all or cover everything?

She chose slacks, a modest blouse and blazer. No perfume today. Looking in the mirror she said aloud, "upscale frumpy."

She ate a banana, drained the last of the coffee and reluctantly walked out to her car.

Burke ran his thumb over the gold letters of B.T. Development on the door. He had never noticed the small chip on the B. Sober faced he opened the door and saw Veronica leaning into the drawer of a filing cabinet. He watched her for a moment then closed the door to break the silence.

"Good morning. Where is everyone?" *He asked, looking around.*

"It isn't nine o'clock yet. You're early." *She didn't look at him.*

"Can we have coffee in my office?"

"Sure. Can I pull the bid I'm looking for? I'll be there in a minute."

She bent over the drawer to stall long enough to compose herself and hoping he didn't want to have 'the conversation,'

Burke went into his office, opened the blinds and looked out the window. She came in and sat the cups on the coffee table and sat in the middle of the couch, giving the impression she was not giving room for him to sit beside her.

He sat opposite her, they drank without speaking. Suddenly he was on his feet pacing the periphery of the room, over and over again like a caged tiger.

Becoming annoyed, Veronica asked in a harsh tone, "How long are you going to do that?"

He stopped, looked at her with wide eyes and said, "This is crazy. Everything is crazy. I don't know what end is up anymore. My whole equilibrium is shot."

"What's the matter with you? Do I need to call someone?"

"Listen to me for a change."

"For a change?" She almost smiled.

"Whatever. I'm a mess right now. It feels like I'm stuck somewhere between what I want to do and what I've always done."

"I know what you've always done, so what do you want to do?"

"Now you have opened Pandora's Box. You asked the question, do you want the answer?" He was on his feet again.

"Have you thought of taking up jogging to run off some of that energy? Yes I want the answer."

"Here's the thing. This is what I'm almost sure that I want. I want you. Don't say anything. Don't break my stride; I have rehearsed this all night. It drives me crazy that you know me better than I do. Every day I look forward to seeing you. You are impossible sometimes. Even so, I don't know what a day would be like without you here.

"Then, the other issue is those kids. I can't get them out of my mind. My life is out of control and I have never felt more alive. There are more people in my thoughts than just myself for a change. I think I have an idea to pull this all together. There is a chance to build something of substance, not just some glass and steel box that has no lasting reward. I'm still sifting through the details so we'll go over it when I get it all figured out.

"This I do know, I want you to be a major part of it. I want to make this work and I want to be with you." He emptied the coffee in his cup and dropped into a chair exhausted and a bit frightened. At least he had said what he needed to say and it was *time for the chips to fall where they may.*

"Anything else?" Veronica asked, stunned and overwhelmed.

"No, that's about it for now."

"You have laid a lot on me. I am trying to deal with my own emotions so I can't answer right now."

"Good, because either way I couldn't handle it."

"You're pitiful," She laughed.

"I know and I don't care."

At that moment she fell more in love with the blob in the chair than she had been with the Burke of two weeks ago. The man she saw today was someone she had never met.

For more than two weeks Posy and I slept in the cramped storeroom with boxes of toilet paper and napkins. We were grateful but there was absolutely nothing homey about it.

One day when we were out walking around the neighborhood we saw a sign in the window of an old apartment building that read, 'For Rent, Studio Apartment'

"Look, look at that," Posy screamed.

"Let's go look at it. What's a studio apartment?"

"I don't know, let's go find out."

We opened the door and saw the sign on the first apartment that said, "Manager" We knocked and a very large man with a scruffy beard and a cigar in his mouth opened the door and said, "What can I do for ya?"

"We are inquiring about the apartment," I smiled.

"Rents two hundred dollars a month, first month in advance and a hundred dollar deposit. No pets, no loud music, no wild parties. Do you want to see it?"

"Yes please." Posy was trying to contain herself.

"Hang on, I'll get the key."

We followed him up two flights of stairs and down the hall. It was clean and well lit. He stopped at number 209, unlocked the door and stepped aside to let us go in first.

It was a large room with windows on one wall. There was a small kitchenette with a refrigerator, small stove, sink and an island counter separating it from the room. The bathroom was small but had a tub and shower. Considering where we had come from, this was like a palace. The best part was the floor had carpet.

"Do you pay utilities?" Posy asked.

"Water and power, you pay for a phone if you want one, and the trash; the pickup is every Monday. I'll step out in the hall. Talk it over."

We stood in the middle of the room. The light from the large windows was warm and cheerful. I saw a door next to the bathroom door. I opened it, it was a closet.

"Check this out, no more boxes or backpack, no more wrinkles. Can we afford this? He wants three hundred dollars right off the bat."

"With our savings and our jobs I think we can swing it. We will just have to be careful."

"We know how to do that," I laughed.

"We are going to have to open a bank account one of these days."

"About time to play grown-up I guess." I felt a little sad.

We opened the door into the hall. He was leaning against the wall. He stood up straight when he saw us.

"We'll take it. We can move in this weekend if that's all right with you."

"That's fine. Pick up the key then."

We couldn't wait to tell Trudy that she was getting her storeroom back. We ran back to the café and told her the news. She was very excited for us. She offered to give us the roll-away bed and even offered to have her husband deliver it.

Saturday evening after work we moved into our first home. Trudy and her husband, Larry, came with the bed and all our boxes. They parked in the street and we quickly unloaded everything and piled it on the sidewalk. It took the four of us to carry the bed up the stairs and we had to stop midway to catch our breath and shuffle positions so the load wasn't going to kill us all at once.

When we walked into the apartment Trudy said with a big smile, "Wow, I hope you don't go blind with all this light after living like bats for so long. This is just great."

After we finished bringing up all the boxes Larry brought in another large box.

"Here is a little something we thought you might need. It's a house-warming present."

We looked inside and found a coffeepot, coffee, and a whole pie from the café, coat hangers and toilet paper.

"I was going to have a garage sale one of these days and I have some lamps, end tables, a couple of chairs and odds and ends that you might just as well have if you want. It would save me the hassle of having to sit in my front yard all day listening to people haggle." Trudy smiled at Larry.

"Besides, I have been waiting years to be able to park in the garage. We could bring stuff over tomorrow if you don't have plans."

Posy looked at me, "So, do we have plans?"

"I don't have plans."

"Fantastic. You have saved my life. See you around noon." Larry said.

We gave them both a big hug. "I think its visa-versa on the saving your life thing. Thank you so much. For everything." I was about to cry.

When they left we sat on the bed and just looked around the room before we started to unpack the boxes.

The next morning we had pie and coffee for breakfast. Larry and Trudy arrived carrying lamps and more boxes. We helped them bring up two chairs, a chest of drawers, and two end tables. We had furniture!

They didn't stay long so we had the rest of the day to arrange everything and to go to the store and buy some small groceries.

When we put the milk, lunch meat and bread in the refrigerator Posy said, "Is that just too cool or what?"

"Yep but you know what's really cool? Having drawers for our underwear."

"Yeah but you know what's super cool? I found out there is a laundry room in the building. We don't have to wash our clothes in the bathtub anymore."

"No way, man it doesn't get any better."

The next afternoon after work I went to the gallery to tell them I had moved. When I walked in, Veronica was the first thing I saw. I quickly turned to leave but she saw me before I could get out the door.

"Wait, don't leave. Please, I have to talk to you." She bolted toward me like a jackrabbit.

"What could you possibly have to say to me? I came to talk to him." I pointed to the owner.

"Hi Hope, how's it going?" He smiled.

"Oh, just ducky, thank you. By the way did she happen to mention that her boss blew my building to smithereens? Now she want's to talk to me. I came by to let you know I was forced to move, which really turned out o.k. in the long run but it was quite awful for awhile. So, how are the bags doing?"

"We only have three left."

"Hope, Burke want's to see you," Veronica broke in.

"Excuse me, I'm doing business here. Anyway, we all know what Burke wants, Burke gets. He got what he wanted. Why would he want to see me? I'm just part of the debris he had to sweep up."

"No, I don't think he got what he wanted. He asked me to find you so he could finish the conversation he started with you before. He wants to talk to both you and your friend."

"We'll talk it over, but don't hold your breath. As far as we are concerned Burke is the devil himself."

"You still have my card?"

"I still have your card."

I walked slowly toward home, digesting what Veronica had said. I shouldn't get mad at her, it isn't her fault her boss does what he does, I thought.

"How's it going?" I asked when I opened the door. Posy looked over the book she was reading.

"Fine," She said.

"Are you feeling o.k.?"

"Yes, just fine."

"How was your day?" I smiled.

"Just fine, what's up with you?"

"I had an interesting day."

"Really? What did you do?"

"Went to the gallery. They only have three bags left."

"That's great. Does he want more?"

"I don't know."

"You don't know? Didn't you ask?"

"I didn't have a chance. Veronica was there. She said her boss, the creep, wants to see us, both of us."

"You're kidding, right? I'm not going, What could he possibly want from us?"

"I don't know but I'm curious. Come with me, just to check it out."

"Why?"

"Because I'm not going to be intimidated by anyone. I want to look the dragon in the eye. Think of it as a growing experience."

"It's your growing experience, not mine. Besides, wasn't it you that had the dragon by the tail?"

"And now it's time to stand in its tracks and bow before the wounded."

"O.k. I'll go, this might be fun to watch."

He was sitting in the reception area facing the door when we walked in.

"I could have you arrested." He stood up and came toward me. There was no anger in his voice, just a matter of fact statement.

"For what," I said, standing my ground.

"For assault with intent to harm?"

"Fine, call the police. I would love to take you to court, at least to have my say. What is it with you guys anyway? You think just because you are bigger, or stronger, or richer, you can have all the power and can just take what you want, whenever you want it. You loom over the helpless like a mountain. I don't care if it's legal or not, you still steal what doesn't belong to you. What you take, you are not entitled to have."

I was shaking. I needed to get out of there. No one moved. Veronica and Posy looked at me as if they had never seen me before.

"Excuse me, I need a moment." I looked at Burke's ashen face as I ran out the door and down the hall to the lady's room.

In the stall I sat on the john trying to choke back the tears. I began to take deep breaths and clenched my fists. On the outside of the closed stall door I could hear Posy calling me. She sounded scared.

"Not now, just leave me alone for a second."

"Ok." She closed the bathroom door behind her.

I blew my nose, threw my head back and counted the tiles on the ceiling. The anger that I had pushed down so deep for so long erupted like a latent volcano. I didn't know it had been festering all these years. I was ashamed and frightened. Burke wasn't my father and I had no right to purge all over him another time. Splashing cold water on my face shocked me back to the moment at hand.

He didn't flinch when I walked back into the reception room. The receptionist however made a quick exit like she had a life or death matter that needed her attention.

He looked at Veronica, "Could we have some coffee in my office please? Bring four cups and some of those sinfully chocolate cookies."

In his office we sat on the couch. He was more relaxed in jeans and a T-shirt. He kicked off his shoes and put a cookie in his mouth.

I saw the opportunity to say something; "I want to apologize. That came out of nowhere, just past stuff that doesn't belong to you."

"Apology accepted. Now here's the thing. I'm going through a metamorphosis or something, or maybe I have lost my mind all together. Anyway, I'll cut to the chase. I have money and I know people." He looked at me, "You have talent," then to Posy, "you have assets you don't even know about yet."

Posy looked at Veronica, "What does she have?"

He looked at Veronica and his eyes softened, "Everything."

He got up and walked around the room. It was amusing to see him padding around in his stocking feet.

"Seems to me that we have a team here. I'm willing to put up the money to go into business with you. I have a vacant warehouse that I was going to convert into condos and put retail business spaces on the street level. It is big, open and full of potential. Posy, you have some great sales ability."

He looked at me and started laughing, "I'm almost ready to offer to send you to law school, just kidding, don't hit me again, I'm just beginning to heal. You're some piece of work, but I'll say this for you, if you put your talent to serious work it's no telling what you could accomplish."

"Slow down, wait a minute," I interrupted. "What's in this deal for you? There's no free lunch anywhere."

"This is an investment for me. I'm a businessman; I know an opportunity when I see one. I take ten percent until my investment is paid off, after that the books should be in the black and I will take five percent of the profits. That's it."

"You will be in our faces telling us what to do all the time."

"The last thing I want to do is be in your face all the time. I'll show up once a month for a business meeting, if you want to talk to me in between, hunt me down. Otherwise, I'm out of your life. I suggest Veronica work with you. She knows how to work with people, you could learn a lot from her."

"Hold on Burke, what makes you think I want to work with these pint-sized commandos. Who is going to work my job at B.T. Development?"

"I don't know. Maybe you could split your time between the two; those are details we will have to work out. This is our first brainstorming session, we don't have to figure everything out today."

After the meeting we had the cab take us to the café. We needed to talk to Trudy. There were no customers and it was close to closing time. She put the CLOSED sign in the window and poured us coffee.

After we told her about Burke's offer she said, "What do you want to do?"

"I don't know. As long as a dream lies dormant, fear is never part of the equation."

"I never had a big dream. I only hoped to eat everyday. Now suddenly I'm in the middle of your dream and I don't know what my place is." Posy looked out the window.

"So what are you afraid of?" Trudy persisted.

"Everything. What if I can't do it? Then it all blows up and Burke is out a lot of money. I'm afraid of loosing my freedom. Everything is going to change."

"Not that you asked what I think, but this is what I think. For whatever reason you both flew the coop looking for something better. Maybe you think what you have is better than what you left, and maybe it is but it could be better still. Do you really want to wait on tables the rest of your life? Do you think you are going to be twenty years old forever? Everyone thinks they are going to be twenty forever. Then one day they realize they can look back on their twenties and it seems like light-years ago.

"You can't go backwards, and you can't stay stuck where you are. The only direction you can go is forward into the future. You might consider that the biggest blessing you received was the day that building went down. Sometimes the path isn't in a straight line. Hope, get over yourself, this isn't all about you. Posy, maybe it's time you step up to the plate. Anyway, what's the worse that can happen? If it doesn't work out you end up right back here."

"What if….." I started to say.

"No, you're stuck. Turn the 'what if' coin over. What if you make it? What if you're happy? Now get out of here, go talk. I have work to do."

She got up and went into the kitchen. I picked up the cups and took them in and washed them. Trudy didn't look at me.

"I'll see you in the morning," I said.

"See you then."

Posy and I walked along the waterfront without talking to each other. There was a chill in the air and it wasn't the weather. The sun was going down behind the mountains. We sat on a bench and looked across the Sound.

Posy turned and riveted her eyes on mine. "Did it ever cross your mind that my little life will never be the same either? What really chaps my cheeks is that it is all in your hands. What ever you decide affects me. If you go for it or you don't nothing will ever be the same. It will always be there like a scab. What do I have to offer this situation?"

"This is what you don't get; I'm just the product. Without someone pushing the product, I'm nothing. No one is less or more important than anyone else. Are you forgetting that Burke asked for both of us to come to his office? He has plans for you. Don't think for a teeny second that what you decide to do doesn't affect my little life."

I got up and stood facing the water squelching the urge to bolt. My face was wet. I wiped my face on my sleeve.

"What do you want?" I turned and looked at her.

"I want Malcolm back. I want to take oranges to Auntie Bea and hear her tell me what she thinks I should do. I want to walk into Nordstrom's and feel like I belong there like all the other fine looking people. I want to buy something there like I didn't care how much it cost. I want a big kitchen with so much food in the cupboard that I have to stand there looking at it before I decide what to cook." Her voice was shaking as the tears came.

"I know, me too."

"Come with me, I want to show you something," She said.

We walked a block south and stood in front of the market. She pointed to Pike Street. "See that hill? At the top is another level of the city and the second hill takes you to even another and better level. Yeah, it looks like a mountain from here but it can be climbed."

I looked up the street. "I can't see the top," I whispered.

"No, but from the top you can look back and see forever. Maybe we could just go look at Burke's building."

The next day after the lunch crowd had cleared out I called Veronica and asked when would be a good time for us to come look at the building. I made it clear that we just wanted to see it, no strings attached. She put me on hold and came back asking if we could meet her and Burke there that afternoon.

We took a bus to Burke's building. It was a large three-story old brick structure with bay windows. On the street level was a bicycle shop called Wheels To Go. The rest of the spaces had "For Rent" signs in the windows. We opened the door to Wheels and went into the store as Veronica instructed. There were bicycles everywhere, the European fancy kind. They were beautiful; bright red, blue and black with sparkling chrome spokes. There were wheels hung all over the walls and signs with names I couldn't pronounce. The air was heavy with the smell of new rubber. It was delicious.

"May I help you?" asked a fine looking young man with a tight T-shirt that didn't camouflage the muscles under it, asked with a smile.

"No, just looking around. We are meeting someone here."

"Do you like bikes?"

Posy lit up, "I do. You sure have some beauties."

"We build custom bikes to order, that's the fun part."

"You ladies interested in real-estate?" A familiar voice asked. We turned to see Burke coming through the door.

"No, just looking," Posy repeated.

"Well then, let me give you the dollar tour. Nice bikes, huh? This is Richard, a fine craftsman. Richard, this is Lucy and Ethel."

"Which is which?"

"Depends on the day and the full moon."

"Nice to meet you both, who ever you are," Richard smiled but clearly kept his gaze on Posy.

Burke led us to the door next to the bicycle shop. Once inside the main entrance we stood looking at the natural brick walls and the wide oak staircase winding to the second floor. The tall windows facing the street were arched at the top. Light flooded the open space. The floors were worn, giving the wood a warm patina.

I was dazzled. All of my artist senses were at their highest pitch. I laughed at Posy standing there with her mouth open, wide eyed, as she seemed to be thrown into a state of shock.

"Shall we go upstairs?" Burke smiled.

We followed him to the second floor. My hand slid along the oak banister. It felt like silk. The top of the stairs ended at the entrance to an enormous room. The whole top floor was open without interior walls. The perimeter walls were also brick. The ceiling went up past the windows that appeared to be meant to be a third floor.

I sucked in air and made a choking sound. I could almost hear an echo. Shafts of light created a patchwork across the floor and up the brick walls.

"Well, what would you do with this place?" Burke turned

and looked at us.

"You're the developer," I said.

He looked at me. "Tell me what you see, not now, but finished. Draw me a picture in your mind."

I walked to the middle of the room feeling like a gnat on the beach. Raising my arms above my head and looking up I turned around in a circle, taking in the total space in motion.

"You could be a contender!" Posy yelled, her voice bouncing off the empty space.

I sat down on the floor and pulled my knees up under my chin.

"Give me your best shot," Burke said.

"Cat walk."

"What?"

"Offices, but open on the front, glass doors. All along the walls, a catwalk like a loft looking down on the main floor."

"And down here?"

"Studio, work space and lunch room and bathrooms."

"What about the entry?"

"Couches and tables, like a front room. The reception area, a place to meet people, and big plants or trees by the big windows. The receptionist desk in the corner faces the door.

"Well, well, I think you might be on to something."

"It's a lot of money," I said.

"Not too much, but you might want to add something."

"What?"

"How about an apartment up there, a place to live while

the business grows," he pointed to the area that was to be the upper level.

"Are you serious?" Posy screamed.

"I'm so serious."

"We can help build stuff, we are good with our hands," Posy said.

"So, are we in business then?"

"Seems like we are."

"Excellent. Do you think you could draw out some kind of floor plan showing what we talked about, then meet back here in two weeks to go over things?"

"Sure," I said. "I think I can do that."

"Very good, see you then." He shook our hands and the commitment was made.

Burke felt lost without Veronica. She had been out of the office for three days with a cold.

"Hello," she sneezed into the phone.

"You called?" Burke asked.

"No," she sniffed.

"Really? You didn't call?"

"I didn't call, why would I call?"

"To thank me for the roses for one thing."

"What roses?"

"The ones being delivered in five minutes."

"Really?" Her scratchy throat could not conceal her surprise.

"Truly."

"You said, 'for one thing.' What's the other thing?"

"That's none of your business." He smiled to himself; maybe he had the last word this time.

"Cute," she said as the doorbell rang.

"Thanks in advance, for one thing," she hung up the phone before he could say anything.

He held the receiver for a moment and laughed, his moment of victory was short but worthy. Just as soon as he put the receiver down the phone rang.

"Hello," He said, a bit irritated.

"They are gorgeous, they are yellow, my favorite."

"I know."

"How do you know that?"

"You mentioned it once,"

"You amaze me."

"Get well and quit oozing."

"Bye," She hung up the phone and tried to smell the roses.

He hung up, leaned back in his chair and smiled, remembering the past weekend. They had talked on the phone for almost an hour on Saturday night. They didn't discuss business but talked about get acquainted subjects.

He picked her up on Sunday morning. They went to breakfast, then took the ferry to Bainbridge Island.

They rode outside watching the city skyline recede. Veronica wore jeans, a sweater and tennis shoes. He had never seen her dressed casually and the way her hair blew freely gave her a little girl look that warmed his heart. When they threw chips up to the seagulls flying alongside the boat, the birds swooped down and grabbed them in mid air. They laughed like delighted children.

When the ferry docked they walked toward the small shops with the rest of the tourists. Burke watched the people strolling on the sidewalk.

"So this is what people do on Sundays," he said with a sad tone.

"What do you mean?"

"People do stuff on Sunday. What do you do?"

"I have stuff to do, like laundry and dusting. What do you do?"

"Depends on the season."

"What?"

"Well, there's football, baseball, basketball and golf on TV. That pretty much wipes out the whole year.

"So in other words, you sit on your butt for a year of Sundays and watch other people doing stuff?"

"We're pathetic."

"Yes, we are."

He took her hand as they walked, "Let's get crazy and eat ice-cream."

They took the ferry back to Seattle. Their mood was more subdued, a bit sad that the day had to end, yet full of contentment that they couldn't verbalize. It was twilight when the skyline came into view and lights began to twinkle in the windows of the buildings, casting little diamonds onto the water.

After the ferry docked at the terminal they went to the parking lot to Burke's car and he drove Veronica home. He parked in her driveway. Neither of them moved.

"You have never seen my pad, would you like to come in and

have a cup of coffee for the road?"

"That would be nice."

When they walked in her front door Veronica turned on the light in her front room. Burke was surprised at what he saw. The room was immaculate with a large white couch sporting pastel green and peach toss pillows. The chairs were patterned in green and light brown. The white book shelves were full of books and small collectibles. The white marble fireplace showed signs of use. He followed her into the small but efficient uncluttered kitchen. He stood in the doorway and watched her fill the coffeepot. Soon the smell of warm, sweet fresh-brewing coffee was in the air, filling him with a comforting glow.

She poured the cups and handed him one. They went into the front room and sat on the couch.

"I'm impressed," he said looking around the room.

"Why?"

"Because it looks just like you, warm and classy."

He finished his coffee and stood up. "I have to go now, I'm getting far to comfortable."

She walked him to the door. They stood there for a moment. She reached up and stroked his cheek. He bent down and gently kissed her.

"I had the best time, thank you so much," she said.

"Thank you back. What a scrumptious day." He kissed her on the top of her head and walked out the door.

He tried to sleep that night. He couldn't get his pillow right. He pounded it, turned it over, folded it and finally threw it on the floor. The clock on the bedside table said 2:12 a.m He got up, *went into the kitchen. He opened the refrigerator door; there was nothing in it except two stale donuts and a quart of milk. He took a big gulp of the milk, it was sour. He spit it into the sink and rinsed out his mouth directly from the faucet.*

He walked around his town house as if he had never been there before. For the first time he was aware of how austere it was. There was nothing personal about his surroundings that spoke of who he was. He wondered how long the dead plant had been dead. He couldn't remember ever watering it, or even when he had acquired it. He touched the brittle leaves, Veronica would have watered it, he thought. She nurtured things, she made things grow. He threw the plant into the trash and went back to bed.

He stretched his arms above his head, got up from his chair and tried to return to the moment. It had been an eye-opening weekend he realized. He knew that when Veronica got well and returned to work, he had to tell her that he loved her.

PART THREE

With Veronica looking over his shoulder, Burke intently looked at my drawing, taking his time to go over every detail. At last he looked at me and shook his head.

"Very impressive. Where did you learn how to do this?"

"Just common sense, space is space," I said.

Burke smiled. "My favorite part is the way you segregated the work areas and put counter space along the outside walls to save square footage. The only thing you need to do is to connect the plumbing. See, this bathroom needs to be moved so it is by this bathroom and the lunchroom. Then the upstairs bathrooms and kitchen need to be above the lower plumbing so it connects to their system. If we don't have the pipes all strung out it will save money. Also if there is ever a problem it will be easier to find."

"That makes sense. Is there anything else that you see?"

"I will have to adjust some support walls under the balcony of the upper offices, but that's just a few details. Let me take care of the electrical, I know about that part. I'm thinking we should be able to start construction in the early fall. That will give us time to get the blue prints drawn up and get the crew together. I need to get someone in here to clean up the place. Anyone have any questions?"

"I do, I have been worried that I'm not going to make bags fast enough if this thing flies like we seem to think it will. It takes time and I can't just whip them out in the blink of an eye."

"I thought about that. I checked into a printing press. We can get one for a reasonable price. That way we can mass produce each design and we can also do other things like stationery, cards and other paper products."

"That takes a load off my mind. I'll be able to get some designs done between now and then."

"Great. We have a plan then," Burke said and moved toward the door. I heard him ask Veronica to dinner.

Posy and I stood at the bus stop in front of the building. The late afternoon sun was bright on our faces.

Posy was grinning, "Are you excited?"

"I'm so excited I can't stand it."

The bus stopped, we got on and sat in the back where we could be alone in case one of us needed to scream.

"You know what impressed me most about him, he didn't take over like a big shot. He listened. I think there's something going on between him and Veronica," I said.

"Really?"

"Seriously, didn't you notice how they looked at each other?"

"That would be nice."

"I think today was the turning point. We have just entered the human race. We need to get legal and open a bank account like we talked about. It can't be put off any longer. What that means is we have to put our given names on the dotted line. I'm sure Burke is going to have some kind of legal papers drawn up and they will need to be signed. So, who are you, legally speaking?"

"I will always be Posy, but from the worlds point of view I'm Elizabeth Wallace. There you have it. And who might you be?"

"Hope Turner. Just from a curiosity standpoint, where are you from?"

"I'm from Nebraska."

"No kidding, I'm from Kansas, we are neighbors," I said and slapped her on the back.

"People back there have there own way of looking at things. Maybe that's why we understand each other."

That was all that needed to be said.

The next morning when I went to work Trudy looked at me and said, "Don't we look smug, what's going on?"

"It's happening. We went and saw the building yesterday. It's fabulous. I'm going to do it Trudy, I'm going to be a business woman."

"Well look at you. I am so proud of you. I have to say that I hate to loose you though. Tell me everything. When is this going to happen?"

I gave her all the details then tried to make her feel better. "It won't be until the fall and I don't know how long it will take for the construction to be finished. You are stuck with me for awhile. Anyway, that is after the tourist season."

She nodded and we hugged and said good-bye.

After the meeting, Burke and Veronica left the building. In the car Burke said, "I think we have a winner here. Those kids are eager to learn and seem to be flexible enough to work with, not to mention a kick in the pants."

"They are pretty cute all right. I think Hope's talent will mature into something strong. I look forward to taking Posy under my wing and show her the ropes of selling. She is hard to turn down when she makes up her mind to something and that is a positive thing if challenged in the right direction."

They drove to the Thirteen Coins and sat in one of the private booths toward the back. They watched the frenzied chefs behind the counter preparing meals. They dodged and weaved around each other like a culinary ballet. Once in awhile flames would shoot up from something sautéing on the large stove.

"I wonder if they carry fire extinguishers on their belts," Veronica laughed.

After they ordered Burke knew his time was looming. He noticed his palms were beginning to sweat.

"How are you feeling?" He asked.

"Much better, not a hundred percent, but better."

"That's good, I was concerned about you."

"That's nice to know."

"I have something I need to say Veronica. I had time to think about many things while you were out of the office. Mostly, I missed you. Veronica, I love you."

"You asked me once who I loved. I guess it's time to make it your business, you, I love you."

"I knew it, I just knew it," he almost yelled.

The waiter came with their food and they ate between grins at each other. There was no conversation until the coffee and chocolate cake came.

"I think we should go steady," Burke said.

Veronica almost choked on her cake. "Go steady, how high school of you."

"No, really. We need to see where this will take us."

"Does that mean that I have to get rid of those fifteen hunks that are clamoring at my door every night?"

"Do you want to get rid of them?" he laughed.

"I don't know, I'll get back to you on that."

"I didn't notice, do you have live plants inside your house?"

"Yes, I have live plants inside my house, why?"

"Nothing. How are they doing?"

"They are doing just fine. You are really weird Burke. You do know that don't you?"

"Yes I do. That's why we need to get to know each other before I ask you to marry me. We probably both have a few ways that we are set in, good to know those things before we spend a lot of money on those little sandwiches without the crusts."

"What sandwiches without crusts?"

"The ones they always serve at wedding receptions."

"Did I miss something here? Did you ask me to marry you?"

"No. I meant if I ever do, if we still like each other when we know more than we do now."

"*Take me to my car.*"
"*Ok.*"

Posy and I began the process of legitimizing ourselves. We took most of the cash from the coffee can and opened a checking account at the nearest bank.

I went to the gallery to tell Randy that he could start paying me by check. He then told me that he needed at least a dozen more bags. When I told him what was going on with Burke he was ecstatic.

"Veronica has been a good customer for a long time. This is great news; you will be on the map before you know it. We should think about having a show for you next summer."

"Right now I can't fit anything else into my head. I'll get the bags to you as soon as I can."

The next two weeks were put on a tight schedule as I learned the squeaky wheel concept. After work I surrounded myself with bags, pens and tape spread out over the kitchenette counter. Posy took up cooking and laundry. Eventually her job at the market would be over when the vendors packed up their wares for the winter. For now, the tourists were buying up everything in sight. She continued her paper route, knowing it would be there when nothing else was.

The summer light began to be lower and the days were becoming shorter. There was that unexplainable feeling in the air that warned of approaching autumn, even though the leaves showed no indication of ever turning. The dog days of summer were upon us and I just wanted to throw it a bone to keep it around as long as possible.

I finished the bags in less time than it to took me to do the first ones. The floor plan drawing was redone.

I called Burke and he agreed to meet me at the gallery to save me two trips. He was there when I arrived.

"Let's see what you've done," Randy said.

Both of them looked through the fifteen bags that were spread on the counter. All of them were different.

Burke seemed surprised. "Now I have seen more of what you can do, and I am very impressed."

Randy smiled in agreement. "The girl can produce."

"Thank you both, I appreciate it," I said with a sigh of relief.

"Let's go grab a cup of coffee," Burke said to me.

Randy gave me a check and we went next door to a small café with tables outside on the sidewalk. We picked one in the sun.

I showed him the revised floor plan. He studied it carefully and grinned.

"That's the ticket."

He laid it aside, looked me square in the eye and said, "So, how are you doing? I mean really doing." He was serious.

"It depends on the moment. I'm overwhelmed, afraid I won't be able to keep up the pace and produce enough variety, I'm excited and I greatly appreciate your taking a chance on me. I'm worried about your huge investment. It feels like it all falls on me, if people don't like my work, you loose a boatload of money. It's almost impossible to focus on anything right now. Other than that, I'm just fine."

"Well, you know what, if you didn't feel all of those things, I would be the one to be really worried. This might be the most major step in your life so far. It might be good not to look at everything all at once. You put a puzzle together one piece at a time."

"Someone said almost that same thing to me once, only put differently."

"I wouldn't want to be involved if I wasn't reasonably sure there was a good chance for success."

"Are you using me to clear your conscious?" I asked bluntly.

"I don't know. Maybe a little, but mostly I want to do something a hundred degrees from what I have done most of my life, something that I can have fun doing for a change. I want to put my money into something rewarding. The way I see it is that you give me a chance to change my life and I do the same for you. It's a win-win situation."

"Thank you for being honest, that makes me trust you easier."

"Everyone has something unique to offer, that's why I am optimistic it will be a success."

"Thanks Burke, I feel better."

"Good. It looks like the crew will be on board as soon as I get the draftsman's finished blueprint. Looks like we can begin in a few weeks. We can all get together then and see how things are progressing. We will also talk about money at that time. I think you and Posy should be put on salary as soon as we start production and get things put together to start a product line. Oh, by the way, I think Richard at the bicycle shop has a crush on Posy. He was asking about her the other day."

"No kidding."

"He wanted to know if she would go out with him, maybe for lunch."

"He should ask her."

"I'll tell him. I guess that's about it. Call me in a couple of weeks, it was good talking with you Hope. Take care."

We tried to hang on to the familiar of what was while we waited for the next phase of what was to come.

One night I said to Posy, "Your birthday is coming up, what would you like to do?"

"Nothing. Nothing could compare to last year."

"That was something all right. Auntie Bea was so excited."

"The anniversary of her death isn't that far off. I just hope it doesn't snow on that day, I couldn't take it." She looked down at the floor and her shoulders drooped as if feeling the weight of sadness.

"How did you meet her?" I had always wondered.

"About a year before you came along I was walking around lost and frightened. I had just arrived in the city. I ended up under the viaduct and there she was, singing her heart out, 'Just a closer walk with thee.' I was mesmerized. I just stood there listening to her and when she saw me she motioned for me to come to her. She opened her arms and welcomed me. I lived there for quite a while.

"She was the mayor and pastor of that little village and she ran a clean ship. She wouldn't allow anyone on drugs, no drinking or fighting. She would say, 'Poor don't mean down and out.' Once a guy, strung out on something, pulled a knife and started charging toward us. Flash came up behind him, kicked him in the back of his knees and dropped him like a rock. Then he picked him up and threw him into the street. Word got out that you don't go under the viaduct if you have trouble in your blood. Some guy made some remarks toward me once and Flash was all over him. Flash appointed himself as my protector, brother and friend. I loved him. I hope he is all right.

"I saw what hungry people look like; it's something in the eyes. It's a haunting vacancy. If anyone scored some food from the mission or from a kind stranger, they shared what they had, when they could have eaten it all. Everyone got a bit of something.

"I made friends with the vendors at the market and talked them into giving me anything wilted or what they couldn't sell. When I brought them vegetables, fruit or bread you would think I was Santa Clause. Do you know how far you can stretch an orange?

"I got the paper route, met the landlord at the market and he rented me the apartment. I had a little money. I began my life, and then you." She was out of breath and took a sip of water.

"I've always wondered why Auntie Bea hoarded all that

money. Do you know?"

"Not really, but I think she was afraid that if she spent a dime she would spend a dollar and Flash wouldn't have a future. I also think she knew she was sick."

There was a box in the closet with my name scribbled across the top. The tape on the flaps had not been removed. I brought it out and sat it at her feet.

"Open it," I said.

She took Auntie Bea's afghan out of the box, wrapped her arms around it and buried her face in it. She began to sob uncontrollably.

"I never want her memory to be something that I have to struggle to retrieve," She said, choking out the words.

"Just listen to her voice in your head. She is singing for Jesus right now. It doesn't get any better than that."

"No, no it doesn't," She almost smiled.

Burke was sitting in the middle of the warehouse when we walked in. He was on an office chair with wheels. He looked up to the ceiling, spun around and held up his hands.

"What are you doing?" I laughed.

"Measuring."

"Measuring what?"

"Empty space."

Veronica arrived with her arms full of paper bags. She sat them down on the card table against the wall.

"What do you have there?" Burke asked.

"Lunch."

We sat down on the folding chairs and ate the sandwiches, chips and cookies. Between bites Burke said, "We have some adjustments to make. That ceiling, as is, would eat us up in power bills in the winter. There needs to be a drop ceiling put over the second level, which could be a storage area over the balcony. The crew is scheduled to show up next week. We are looking at about three months construction time, then moving in, ordering furniture, supplies, setting up the press and so on. So, with no glitches, we should be up and running in January. As soon as we get settled, I want to put Hope and Posy on salary until we are in the black. When everything is rolling, I get lost unless you need me."

He looked at me and winked, "Is that enough information for today?"

"That's enough to digest for now, but I do have a question; are you still planing on putting in the apartment?"

"Sure, why?"

"We can't move in January, it's personal, we just can't." I said.

Posy looked at me as if to say, "Thank You."

"That's fine, what ever you want to do."

"Give us some time to talk."

"Take all the time you need, there is a million things to do in the mean time."

When we got home I made a pot of coffee, took off my shoes, opened the window and curled up on the bed.

"Thank you," Posy said, handing me a cup.

"It's nitty gritty time. We need to lay it all out on the table, and we need to be perfectly honest."

"January is the month Auntie Bea died."

"I know, that's why I said that to Burke."

"I can't be that far away from here then, in strange surroundings and surrounded by distractions. That almost feels like cheating her somehow."

"Neither can I. She needs to be honored properly. I wish we knew where Flash is. That's going to be a hard day for him."

"Do you want to move at all?" She asked out of the blue.

"I don't know, do you?"

"I don't know for sure, I kinda like it here for now."

"Burke's heart is in the right place and there is a lot to be said for no rent and no commute. However, I feel weird about him buying furniture that we use and it isn't ours. Having him front the business is one thing, but our living space is something else again. I don't like being indebted to anyone. The other thing is being in the same building where work is, I need to get away from it sometimes."

"There would always be someone around. This palace may not be much but it is our creation," she said looking over the apartment.

"Yeah, and what if Mr. Fabulous shows up?"

"What Mr. Fabulous?"

"Richard for one, he has a crush on you?"

"Stop it, he does not."

"According to Burke he does."

"Whatever. So we agree to talk to Burke then?"

"Yes, I think so. He needs to know how we feel."

In a few weeks we went to meet with Burke. The warehouse was a mass of activity and full of rolls of wire, pipe, rolls of insulation and piles of lumber and plywood. Workmen were hustling, each doing their own specialty. The power had been connected and table saws were screeching over the sound of hammers. Wall forms were leaning up against the outside walls.

Burke, covered with sawdust waved to us and yelled over the noise. He finished talking to one of the men and walked through the labyrinth toward us.

"Let's get out of here," he said, removing his earplugs.

We sat down at an outside table of the coffee shop. Posy and I were both apprehensive. We didn't know how he would react or respond to the changes we were going to present.

He drank his coffee and listened while we talked through our issues. We laid them out in a matter of fact way and without emotion.

"I understand where you are coming from," he said.

"Is it going to mess up the plans that you have for that space?" I asked.

"No, I think I'll just go ahead and leave it as is. It could be useful as a place to relax, or if someone works late and doesn't want to go home, they can stay over. If by some chance you change your minds, it will be here."

"We thought you might be upset," Posy said carefully.

"I don't get upset often. Anyway, running your life is not my job. I 'm too busy trying to figure out my own."

"Quite impressive up there," I said.

"It's coming along, the next time you see it, it will make more sense. I should get back. Come around anytime you want. As soon as Veronica gets back from visiting her mother in Portland we will get together. I wish you would get a phone so we could be in touch. Take care." He got up, waved and went back to work.

While we were standing at the bus stop Richard came out of the bicycle shop. He was a beautiful creature with a wad of curls on his head, deep dark eyes and a slim but muscular build.

"How are you ladies doing today?" He said in a husky charming voice.

"Fine thanks, how about yourself?" I answered.

"Fantastic,"

"Good," I said.

He looked at Posy. "You like bikes, right?"

"Yeah," she said, looking across the street.

"Come in sometime and I'll show you how we build one from scratch." He shifted his position trying to get her attention.

"Yeah, ok," was her only response.

"Well, see ya then."

"Yeah, see ya."

He gave up and went back into the store.

"What's wrong with you? You can run your mouth like a machine gun. Now your vocabulary is reduced to 'yeah, yeah, yeah, see ya.' If he ever does ask you out, the date would last at tops fifteen minutes before he falls asleep or slams into a coma.

He probably thinks you hate him. I don't believe you."

"Whatever, he is too cute, he makes me nervous."

"You have just kicked Mr. Fabulous in the ego."

"Whatever." She shut the door on the conversation.

Veronica stood in the doorway of Burke's office. He was standing in front of the window looking out at the city. She watched him for a while. What a welcome sight he was.

"Did you miss me?" She asked softly.

He turned slowly with a big grin on his face.

"Horribly," he said, crossing the room to give her a big hug.

"How's your project going?"

"It's going well. We have power and a few support walls up. Posy and Hope don't want the apartment. I think they are overwhelmed with too many changes too fast. They want to stay where they are right now. How's your mother doing?"

"I don't believe anyone thinks their parents will ever grow old. One moment your mother is feeding you strained peas, the next moment you're helping her find her glasses or helping her out of a chair. Neither is prepared to change roles. How do you face the day when she looks at you like you're a stranger?" She started to cry.

"I don't know. What does one do when nothing can be done? We will face that day when it comes." He reached out to her, wanting to offer comfort.

"I'm sorry, it's hard not to be able to do anything to make it better. Can I take you to dinner?"

"No, it was a long drive. I just want to go home, lie in the *tub and go to bed. I just wanted to stop by and see you."*

"I'm glad you did, it's good to have you home." He gave her a quick kiss on the cheek.

Posy and I got through our birthdays without fanfare. We bought a small bookcase at the Good Will Store as our gift to each other. We found some books and a silly ceramic bunny to put on one of the shelves.

The leaves began to turn. The days were becoming short and crisp. As if there was a timer on the sky, the rain came. Only once in awhile the clouds split and let the sun shine through for a brief time. Summer was not quite ready to give in to fall. We had a phone installed with an unlisted number. It made communicating much easier.

Trudy told us that her family was taking her out to dinner on Thanksgiving. They said she spent her days cooking for her customers and she deserved to have someone else cook for her on that day. She invited us to join them. They were going to a turkey house restaurant north of the city. We were honored to be asked.

Trudy, Larry and their little boys picked us up on Thanksgiving afternoon. We drove north on the freeway, giving us a chance to see parts of the city we had never seen. We had a wonderful dinner and enjoyed the children. They were dressed in little suits and acted like grown-ups. Being with them was comfortable and easy. It was good to be with a family.

Suddenly, over night, Christmas lights appeared on the streets, in the trees and in the store windows lighting up Styrofoam snow men and dancing Santa Clauses sprinkled with plastic snow flakes. The city was turned into a mock winter wonderland while shoppers sported umbrellas to keep the rain off their packages. Pink flocking covered Christmas trees, hiding the fact a real tree was under all the sparkle. Brenda Lee belted out Jingle Bell Rock. 'Twas the season to be jolly.'

I went to a Christmas tree lot and found the smallest real green one I could find. When Posy saw it, she laughed.

"Why in the world do people bring trees in the house at Christmas? Where did that come from anyway?"

"I don't know, it's tradition."

"Who started the tradition?"

"I don't know. Scrooge, maybe?"

We tied ribbon on the branches and bought some candles to put on the top of the bookshelf. It was quite festive in a simple way.

One evening Burke called to invite us to a small Christmas party the next afternoon.

"Please come, there will be food and I want you to see the progress we have made, you will be surprised," he urged.

"Ok," I said.

The next afternoon we walked in the front lobby to come face to face with a huge real Christmas tree beside the staircase. We could hear voices and laughter coming from up stairs.

When we climbed the stares and saw the warehouse we came to a screeching halt. It wasn't a warehouse anymore. The balcony was almost done; the bathrooms were enclosed, as was the lunchroom. The room for the press was framed in, waiting for the drywall. The floor was finished with a light gray tile. In the middle of the room was a long table filled with food.

Veronica came to us and gave us a hug, "Merry Christmas," she said more bubbly than usual.

"There they are, our inspiration," Burke said with a big smile and everyone clapped. We had no idea who all the people were. We saw Randy, Trudy and Larry in the sea of faces.

"How did you find Trudy?" I asked Veronica.

"Trudy's Café is in the phone book."

"Wow, this is fantastic."

"I am very impressed," Trudy said when she saw us. She gave us both a big hug and Larry did the same.

We were stunned.

"Come, eat," Veronica said and eat we did. As we were finishing the cold salmon and pate Burke handed us identical red wrapped boxes.

"You didn't say there would be gifts." I was upset.

"There aren't. Open them at the same time."

We tore off the paper, opened the boxes and found a red silk sleep mask inside.

"Just what I always wanted, I have been waiting years for this," Posy said.

I didn't know what to say but did manage a puny 'thank you.'

"Come over here and put them on," Veronica said.

"Are we playing, Pin The Tail on The Donkey?" Posy asked.

"No, just put them on for a minute and I'll let you know when to take them off." She looked at Burke, "I told you this wasn't going to be easy."

Behind the mask and blind I heard sounds I couldn't recognize. Then I heard Veronica say, "Over here, no right there, move in a little closer."

"Ok take them off at the same time, now!"

We removed the masks and we both gasped. I was sure I was going to faint. In front of us, leaning up against the wall was a sign about five feet high and nine feet long. It said, HOPE'S GARDEN. The word garden was spelled out with flowers and vines with butterflies flying around it. The word Hope was painted in Hunter green and edged in gold. At the bottom was a white picket fence.

Richard was standing beside the sign holding onto a bright red bicycle with Posy's name on a big white card hanging from the handlebars.

Posy was trying to breathe and the only thing coming out of her mouth was gasps and, "Oh, Oh, Oh!"

Richard said to her, "I built this for you myself, now will you have lunch with me?"

She went over to him and actually hugged him and said, "I can't believe you did this for me."

I was screaming and jumping up and down. I sat on the floor in front of the sign and touched the flowers. I put my head on my knees and sobbed as I remembered when I made Posy the bag for her birthday, I had told Auntie Bea I didn't have enough money to buy a green pen. Now my name was in green. Posy was standing behind me.

"It is so incredibly beautiful, Hope."

I couldn't answer, I just nodded my head.

When I turned around she was riding her bike around the perimeter; dodging people and laughing like a little kid.

When our craziness subsided Burke introduced us to his friends, some were attorneys, some art collectors, some that had invested in his building projects. He introduced us to the man that had painted the sign. I told him how perfect it was. He said he guessed I liked it when I started crying.

Burke took Veronica aside, "This has to be the best Christmas I've ever had. Do you have plans that you can't break for Christmas day?"

"No."

"Let's go to Portland and spend the day with your mother."

"What? You want me to take you home to meet my mother?"

"Yeah," he grinned.

"Good grief, why would you want to put yourself through that?"

"That's what a gentleman does."

"What does a lady do?"

"Takes her boyfriend home to meet her mother."

"Oh brother! If you can take it, I can."

"Excellent," he said and walked away smiling.

Trudy and Larry offered to take us home, saying they could put Posy's bike in the trunk of their car. People were beginning to thin out as evening approached. Posy and I gave Burke and Veronica a hug.

"There are no words to thank you," I said.

"You shook me to the core," Posy added.

"This is the most fun I've ever had, so thank you back only bigger," Burke said.

Richard came over as we were leaving. He stood in front of us and waited for us to finish our good-byes.

Posy looked at him for a moment. "That was so thoughtful of you. How long did it take you to build it?"

"Off and on, several months in the evenings. It was my pleasure. I was serious, can I take you to lunch sometime when you're here. I like you and would like to get to know you better."

"I would like that, and again, thank you so very much."

"You're welcome, I'll race you sometime."

"Have a good Christmas," Veronica said.

"We did," I hugged them again

We went to church on Christmas Eve. Christmas day we opened our gifts. We gave each other socks, sweaters and candy bars. I gave us a Monopoly game. We made ourselves a dinner of baked chicken and dressing, salad and sweet potatoes. Posy made a pie. We lit the candles and listened to Christmas music on the radio. It was a good day.

Burke picked up Veronica early on Christmas morning. He put her bag of gifts in the trunk along with his and they headed south on 405.

Traffic was light and they were relaxed as they passed Olympia and got closer to Portland. Burke resisted talking about Veronica's mother. He wanted to avoid any preconceptions, one way or the other.

Before they reached the city proper they took the airport exit, and drove along Sandy Blvd. Veronica told him to make a left into a modest well-maintained neighborhood.

"There it is," she said, pointing to a small white house. She felt the jitters coming on. What if her mother didn't like him? What if he didn't like her mother? Worse yet, what if they liked each other?

He parked in the driveway. They unloaded the trunk and rang the doorbell. Veronica took a deep breath and said, "Let's rock and roll."

A small well dressed, white haired lady opened the door. "Come in, Merry Christmas," she said holding the door open.

The house smelled of Turkey and cinnamon. The table was set with holiday plates, and evergreen and floral centerpiece.

Burke sat the bag down and reached out his hand to her, "Merry Christmas Alice, I'm Burke."

"So you're Veronicas young man," she said, giving him a warm handshake.

"I don't know about the young part."

Burke looked around the spotless front room. It was cluttered with a lifetime of memories. Pictures of Veronica showed the span of her life; baby to high school graduation, no teeth to braces to a perfect smile. He pointed to one picture of her as a pre-teen, her hair sticking up all over her head.

"What happened here?" He laughed.

"Well, she took it upon herself to cut her own hair, she wanted to look beautiful for the photographer of school pictures the next day," Alice said shaking her head as if it were one of many frustrations faced by a mother of a precocious child.

"Mother, we don't need to bore Burke with every wobbly step of my childhood," Veronica said.

"She only calls me Mother when she wants to be stern with me," Alice laughed. She went into the bedroom and brought out packages and put them on the coffee table with the others.

"I didn't get a tree, no way to get it home," she said and then began her mother list; how long had they been going together, did he come from a good family, had he been married before.

He answered her questions then took her hands in his, looked her in the eye and said, "I want to ask your daughter to marry me. Do I have your permission?"

"Do you love her?"

"More than I thought I could love anyone."

"Then you have my permission."

Veronica almost dropped her coffee cup, her hands were shaking.

"Burke, what in the world are you doing?"

"I'm talking to your mother, mind your own business," he laughed.

"This isn't my business?" She laughed back at him.

"Not yet."

He reached over to the packages, took a small box and handed it to her. She opened it and saw the sparkling diamond ring *inside. She gasped and looked at him, she was speechless. He took it from her shaking hand and removed the ring.*

"Now it's your business, will you marry me?"

She began to cry. "Yes Burke, yes I will."

"So, does that mean you like me then?"

"A little."

Tears ran down his cheeks as he put the ring on her finger.

"I like your style young man," Alice said.

He kissed her on the top of the head, not wanting to embarrass her or her mother.

"I never thought I would see this day." Alice said, *handing him a package.*

He opened the large bottle of Bay Rum aftershave with the wicker around the bottle.

"Thank you so much Alice, this is my favorite."

He gave her the Este Lauder gift pack with powder, bath salts, lotion and cologne.

"Aren't we going to be the best smelling kids on the block," *she laughed.*

After the gifts of sweaters, sheets, towels and candy had been exchanged, there was one small box left. Veronica handed it to Burke. He opened it and found a small gold pocketknife with his name engraved on it.

"Turn it over," she said.

On the other side it was engraved, 'my love'. All he could do was hug her.

After dinner they helped Alice clean up the kitchen. She put food into plastic containers and put them in paper bags.

"This is for you to take home, I couldn't possibly eat all of this."

"We should be going soon. Thank you for a fantastic day Alice. It was so good to meet you."

"Thank you for coming. Oh my gosh, I'm about to have a son-in-law. What a perfect gift. You kids drive carefully."

They kissed her, said good bye, and loaded the trunk with bags of food and their gifts.

On the freeway, Burke said, "Don't talk to me for awhile, I just want to wallow in my happiness."

"That's just fine, I'm engaged you know," she said looking at the ring on her finger.

They didn't see each other until New Years Eve. He came to Veronica's house and they had Christmas dinner all over again. They drove around the city looking at the lights, went back and watched Dick Clark in Times Square. A New Year had begun.

Posy and I spent New Year's Eve eating chocolate cake and playing Monopoly. Fireworks went off somewhere and we could see the sky burst with color and white sparks exploding and falling. The year was over.

The day of Auntie Bea's death had arrived on a Sunday. We had bought flowers and took them to the waterfront just north of Pike Place Market. We stood on the shore in the rain and placed a flower, one at a time, into the water. We were the only ones there. It was early in the morning, cold and wet. We sang Amazing Grace. The tide was going out, we watched the flowers moving out to sea.

Back home, we warmed up with hot coffee and began talking about her, remembering who she had been.

"She was a magnet," Posy said wistfully. "She drew people to her and they were never the same again."

"It was the love that overflowed from her. She always gave everyone a chance but didn't accept any nonsense."

"That's because she wanted people to bring out the best of themselves and not accept their circumstances. She would say, 'it's not about where you've been, it's about where you're going,' When someone got a job and had to move on, she would celebrate."

"Yeah, she always encouraged me. She showed me that just trying was a success in itself. When I was working on your birthday bag she would get so excited with every flower, which propelled me to keep going. I really don't think any of this would be happening if it weren't for her."

"I know."

"She was a mystery though. Why didn't she ever tell any of us that Flash was her son?" I wondered.

"She was very private, she only told what she wanted you to know."

"Did she ever tell you about her past in Georgia and Chicago?"

"Yes, did she tell you?" She looked at me in disbelief.

"Yeah."

"Why didn't you mention it?"

"Because it wasn't my business. She had a hard life."

"That's a matter of perspective. She was rich in many ways.

She was blessed with the love of a good man and had two sons that adored her. Her parents loved her enough to let her go to something more than they could offer. Her voice brought joy and God to so many lives. There is no way of telling how many people she turned around that might otherwise be dead today. Can any of us hope for more than that?"

"No."

"She will be etched in my heart until I see her again."

We were quiet the rest of the day, everything had been said, every emotion had been felt.

By the end of the month, the new digs for Hope's Garden were almost complete. The walls were up and drywalled. The upper level was in place, including the stairs. The paint crew was scheduled for the first of February. Then the press would be installed. It was becoming more exciting as we approached the time to get down to business.

Veronica called and asked us to come for a meeting the next afternoon. The rain was coming at us sideways while we waited at the bus stop. When we finely got on the bus, it was full of soggy people reeking of wet wool.

We shook ourselves off after we walked in the door. Upstairs we took a tour of the faculty that Burke now referred to as the studio. Counters and worktables were clear of debris, the walls were freshly painted white. Light gray carpet, that matched the floor, had been installed on the stairs. The upper level offices were bare, waiting for furniture. The railing around the upper open walkway was a light oak. The track lighting was bright and cheerful with incandescent and florescent mixed to create natural light.

Clearly, Burke knew what he was doing. We sat down at the large table in the lunchroom. He opened the refrigerator and handed us each a can of pop, he smiled smugly. He was quite proud of himself.

"Did anybody ever think we would get here?"

"Not me," Posy said. There was still a fraction of a splinter between them.

"Why doesn't that surprise me," he laughed.

Veronica sat quietly with her hands in her lap. She was content to give Burke his moment.

"Here's the thing, I sort of misjudged how long things would take, but the good news is, we are slightly under budget, so we have some extra cash if something comes up. So, by the time we order office equipment, get the press installed and so forth we will be into March. Not much happens after the first of the year anyway. We need to get samples and a catalog printed so you and Veronica can go out and sell." He looked at Posy.

"Have you been working on new designs?" He asked me.

"Yes I have. Excuse me for interrupting, but I have an idea. If the press is set up to print bags, stationery and cards, like you mentioned, how about prints? How much would a mat cutter cost? We could mat them and sell them to galleries, gift shops and frame shops. That way, we could maximize each design."

"Absolutely, of course, that's a great idea. What about

frames?" He was on his feet pacing around the table.

"Do we have room for a saw and a work bench?"

"I think we could make it fit, we could put up two walls in the corner of the press room. Do you know how to cut mats and make frames?"

"No, but I can learn to cut mats and we could ask Randy if he knows a framer that would be willing to work a couple of days a week."

He sat down and finished off his drink with one gulp.

"This is fantastic. We could spend a month getting an inventory together. It's not good to try to sell something you don't have yet. People want what they want right then and there. Wait, wait a minute! I just thought of something. There is a small basement under the stairs on the main floor. It's right under the press room. I can have a reverse fan put under the saw, put an air duct in, and have the saw dust sucked from the saw into a container down there and it can be emptied when it gets full. Ok, where was I? Oh yeah, Veronica and I have been talking and we think it would be profitable for all of us to go to New York on a business trip, as well as have some fun while we are there. We can pick up some accounts and see the sights.

"What? You mean all of us?" I asked.

"That's what I mean. New York is full of galleries and shops.

"Unbelievable." Posy put her head down on the table.

"One more thing, Veronica has something she wants to say." She looked like she was about to burst as she waved her hand above her head.

"We're engaged!" She shouted.

"We who?" Posy asked.

"Burke and I, we're engaged."

"Wow, I'm flabbergasted." Posy got up and hit Burke on the back.

"I told you there was something going on between them, I told you," I said.

"How did you know?" Burke acted surprised.

"Ah come on, you have been looking at her like a love sick puppy for months. When are you getting married?"

"In a few weeks. We are going to be married in Portland so my mother can be with us, then we are going to the coast for a few days."

"With your mother," Posy laughed.

"I like her mother, but not that much," Burke said.

They drove to Portland early in the morning, knowing that by the afternoon they would be husband and wife. Alice had made arrangements with her pastor, and they would be married in his church. Veronica had the license and his ring in her purse, he had her ring in his pocket.

"We haven't really discussed where we are going to live," Veronica said.

"How comfortable would you be in my place?"

"Not at all, to be honest. Would you be happy in my place?"

"Yes, I like your place. Mine is just a place to sleep, yours is cozy. I don't have much stuff. Do you have room in your closet for *a few suits and shirts?"*

"We can make room, your suits and my dresses can become friends."

By the time they drove into Alice's driveway they were as giddy as teenagers anticipating their first prom.

When they walked in the door they saw Alice dressed in her finest.

"Don't you look lovely," Burke said, hugging her.

Mother and daughter made eye contact and held it for a long time. The mother knew she was loosing her child and the daughter knew the time was coming when she would loose her mother forever. It was a moment of reconciliation, acknowledgement, and the deepest love between parent and child.

"Don't you ladies get all mushy on me or three of us are going to be a mess," Burke said, knowing they were about to break down."

"Let's go get you two married."

The Pastor greeted them warmly, giving Alice and Veronica a hug and shaking Burke's hand.

The vows were said. Burke put the ring on Veronica's hand and the tears began to roll down his face. Veronica was close to sobbing and Alice was whimpering quietly.

"This has to be the most weepy wedding I have ever preformed, congratulations, you may now kiss the bride."

They went to lunch, took Alice home and headed west to Lincoln City.

They checked into the motel that was right on the beach. From their third story balcony they watched the sunset. It was *more glorious than they could have imagined.*

The next morning, Burke woke up in an empty bed. There was a note on her pillow; 'I have gone to the office to get the continental breakfast, I love you.'

He jumped out of bed and into the shower, amused to finding himself whistling.

He was in a chair reading the complementary newspaper when she came in.

"Good morning, Gwenivere."

"Good morning, Lancelot."

She put the tray full of coffee, Danish and fruit on the table, threw herself into his lap and spoke in a sober tone, looking him directly in the eye.

"There is something I need to tell you."

"What?"

"I'm a married woman?"

"Oh no, I'm married too."

"Happily married?"

"Ecstatically married!"

"Know what else?"

"What?"

"I'm starving to death."

"So am I."

The beach was quiet, just a few of the brave hearts sprinkled across the sand. The season hadn't begun so tourists were few and far between. The morning fog soon dissipated giving the sun a chance to warm the beach.

They ran in the surf, playing tag with the foam. Seagulls

swooped over their heads like little kamikazes as they fought for air space and the chance to grab the flying bread crusts. They played with creepy things in the tide pools beside the rocks. Walking for miles scanning the tide line for shells they found a perfect sand dollar, and stuffed their pockets with shells of all sizes.

They drove south on highway 101 along the coast to Depoe Bay. They watched the fishing boats go out and come in the narrow inlet between the small bay and the ocean. Fishermen cleaned their catch on the docks and packed the fish in ice. At one of the gift shops they found a crystal vase to take home.

Burke looked out to the horizon where the sky was taking on a slight pink cast, the sun was dipping into the sea. He wanted to hold on to every moment but he knew that even perfection has a time limit.

"We could stay a few days longer if you want." He took her hand and held it a little extra tightly.

"It wouldn't make it any easier to leave." She gave his hand a squeeze.

"I guess not."

Departure day had arrived. Veronica shook the sand from their clothes and shoes, packed their bags and they reluctantly checked out. It began to rain as soon as they got into the car.

They didn't talk much on the way home. The music on the radio and the flapping of the windshield wipers said it all.

Burke drove into the driveway. He turned and looked at her.

"Would you like to come in for awhile?" Veronica smiled.

"For how long?"

"For the rest of your life."

On the doorstep he took the key out of her hand, unlocked and opened the door. He scooped her off of her feet and carried her across the thresh-hold. She wrapped her arms around his neck.

"Welcome home Burke," she whispered in his ear.

While Burke and Veronica were gone, I shortened my days at the café, leaving right after the lunch hour, and then going to the studio. Office furniture and supplies had been delivered. The press had arrived, been put together and installed. The press operator that Burke had hired came to oversee the installation.

Richard and Posy were unpacking and knocking down boxes. Piles of file folders, paper, mat board, and various items were segregated in piles on the floor. Desks, chairs and filing cabinets were lined against the outside walls.

From upstairs I heard Posy yell, "Hey, it's the bride and groom."

I leaned over the balcony railing. "Welcome home," I yelled down to them.

"Thanks, what are you guys doing?"

"Some of us have to work," Posy said.

"Oh how I missed that snappy little mouth of yours," Burke laughed.

Over the next few days the piles began to gradually dissipate. I took the corner office space with windows on two adjoining walls, lighting the drawing table from both sides. Colored pens and pencils of every color imaginable were neatly spread out and I had every shade of green nature could produce. The drawers were full of paper.

Posy and Veronica each had an office that was well equipped and ready to become the sales team area.

I stood in the pressroom with anticipation running rampant through me. The sweet smell of ink filled my senses. Sam, the printer operator, was a man of few words but he was a man in charge of his domain as he pushed buttons and loaded paper into the printer.

Suddenly, the big machine began to rapidly spit out paper, one after another. When it was finished, I looked at the print on the paper and saw only yellow blobs splashed in a random pattern. My heart sank. I looked at Sam.

"The colors are laid down one at a time, it's called a four color process. Just wait, it will all make sense soon" he said reloading the first printed-paper back into the machine. When they came out again they were overlaid with magenta and more resembled flowers. When the processes were complete, the prints looked just like the original.

"Well, what do you think?" He asked.

"That's absolutely amazing, I can't believe it."

Prints, brochures, stationery and cards began to pile up on tables in the work area. The brochures had a picture of the sign on the front hunter green cover. We used the image of the sign on the letterhead and a smaller version on the envelopes and business cards. It was official, we were a business.

I struggled with the mat cutter, not able to get clean corners and even edges. The rep from the company came and gave me a crash course; it was all a matter of practice and pressure.

A portfolio was put together, a game plan was in place, and we were ready for New York.

Neither Posy nor I had ever been on an airplane, I hadn't even been to an airport.

We joined the other passengers in line at the check-in counter. People were shoving their luggage with their feet as we moved forward. Children were beginning to become impatient and started running wild around the terminal, having to be chased down by an aggravated parent.

We checked in and walked down the boarding ramp to board the plane. Burke put our small cases and the portfolio in the overhead and we fastened our seat belts.

"Does this mean we're committed?" Posy asked. She looked pale.

"I'm afraid so." I said as the stewardess locked the door.

The plane began to move toward the runway while the stewardess started telling us what to do if the plane crashes. Going through the safety routine, after untangling the tube on the oxygen mask, she put the do-dad over her face and the elastic broke, just as she said, 'in case of an emergency'. She chuckled and reassured us that they had more of them. I could only hope that the ones in the compartment above our heads were the new ones.

She described the Emergency Exits; two forward, two aft, and one over each wing.

I took note that I was in a window seat over a wing and

I felt much better for a moment before I panicked. If my seat belt stuck, I would be trampled to death by bodies climbing over me to get out. I also knew that on the food chain of life, Posy and I were on a far lower rung than Veronica and Burke would save her first.

Hanging on to the armrests, as the plane picked up speed, I looked out the window for a split second. The nose of the plane shot upward and the ground dropped out from under us.

"Oh man, we're in the air. This thing is flying." I looked at Posy, she was frozen.

I closed my eyes. I was scared to death. My body was pushed to the back of my seat.

When the plane leveled the captain's voice came over the speaker to tell us that we would be flying at forty three thousand feet, and we were free to get up and walk around.

"Why do we need to know the altitude? So we will know how long it will take to hit the ground if this thing falls out of the sky?" Posy asked.

"Shut up," I said.

Burke and Veronica were across the aisle from us chatting like they were oblivious.

The stewardess gave us food of some sort and drinks. The longer we flew east the darker it got. I tried to wad up the teeny pillow so I could sleep but it never happened.

The pilot announced that we would soon be landing in New York in about an hour and that we would begin our descent. The plane began to slow down, and my nerves began to speed up again. Shortly the nose pointed down and I heard a strange sound.

"What's that?" I yelled to Burke.

"The flaps are going down, they are on the wings and slow down the plane, like brakes."

Before long I saw lights below us and the pilot told everyone to take their seats. I heard a thump as the lights got closer to the belly of the plane.

"That's the wheels going down," Burke volunteered.

Suddenly, the lights were off the wings and we were on the ground. Then there was a sound and we jerked forward. The man beside Posy told us that the engines had been reversed to slow the plane. That made no sense to me what so ever.

We were at the gate, the doors were opened and I wilted. By the time we departed and walked into the airport terminal my legs were functioning again. We collected our luggage and went out to catch one of the hundreds of yellow cabs along the curb.

My illusion of regained safety was short lived. The cab driver threw our bags into the trunk. Right off the bat he started honking at anyone in front of him. He pushed down on the throttle and didn't let up. Burke told him where we were going, and informed him that he knew the city.

As soon as the driver got on to the Long Island Expressway he weaved in and out of the heavy traffic at full speed.

The wall of lights of Manhattan were suddenly in front of us as we crossed the bridge over the East River. The buildings seemed to float above the reflections in the water.

We arrived at our hotel. The lobby was small without amenities. We went to the eleventh floor in one of the two elevators.

Posy's and my room was adjacent to Burke and Veronica. We unpacked, freshened up and found a deli down the street. We had a small dinner, all that was wanted was sleep.

We chose which bed we wanted. I opened the window and laid down on my bed under the window. This was truly the city that never sleeps. Even from eleven floors above the street, sirens, honking horns and screeching tires managed to infiltrate our futile attempt to sleep.

In the morning Veronica knocked at our door, we were up and dressed. When we walked out onto the street, the wide sidewalk was full of people, shoulder to shoulder. It didn't take long to see that the pedestrians walked faster than the traffic moved in the streets. They moved half-sprinting, bodies ramrod straight and not making eye contact. Like trying to enter the freeway at rush hour, we tried to join the mass but we weren't up to speed. The alternative was to stay close to the buildings, or the slow lane, to avoid being crushed.

When they came to a crosswalk they halted at the No Crossing light. When it changed people bolted into the street going in four different directions to join the other masses on the other side. Every kind of dress ran the gambit, from rags to mink.

An old woman pushing a shopping cart, full to the brim, slowly passed us. Bent over the cart handle, she didn't look at anything but the sidewalk. She was dressed in layers, a ragged denim coat over a cardigan sweater over a plaid work shirt. Her tennis shoes were little more than laces and soles, exposing her dirty crusted bare feet. Within a block we saw a half-dressed man sleeping in the shade of a building. No one paid any attention to them, no one stopped. We just walked on by with everyone else. Posy looked at me briefly; I saw it in her eyes, the look of acknowledgment.

I looked down, trying to compose myself, and saw hands holding designer handbags, briefcases, and cameras. Was I becoming one of them I wondered?

We found a small, well-populated restaurant and waited for a table listening to the waitress, the cook and the customers yelling full volume at each other. Every voice was trying to be heard.

Seated and given coffee, we took a vote on what to do with the day. Veronica wanted to ride the subway. Thankfully Posy was far from receptive, giving me an opportunity.

"I don't go into caves," I said.

"It's not a cave, it's mass transportation."

"The key word there is 'mass', mass in a tube, in a cave." I was emphatic.

"I prefer to stay above ground and take my chances with the crazy cab guy, at least I can see where I'm going." Posy said backing me up.

From the top of the Empire State Building the magnitude of the city could be seen from all around the observation deck. It was hard to comprehend how many people were living their lives below. How many old people were shoving shopping carts looking for their place of respite? How many men, mothers with children were lost? Not one of them had an Auntie Bea living in their heart or had a Burke, a Veronica or a Posy standing by their side. Gratitude and guilt make a strange cocktail I thought, but it was a potion that I had for breakfast every day. But today I stood above it all, looking over the top of the haze.

We returned to street level and began the walk toward uptown. Around the outside edges of Rockefeller Center Veronica saw two shops that she thought would be a good match for Hope's Garden. Burke had been toting the Portfolio all day just in case a possibility arose. We sat at an outside coffee shop while Veronica and Posy took the portfolio into the shops.

"This is killing me, not knowing their reaction. What's taking them so long, I've already had three cups of coffee." I looked around, trying to see them.

"Settle down. It's better for them to make the calls without you. Veronica can sell you better than you can. Posy needs to learn how to talk to customers, this is a great opportunity for her. Besides, Veronica is the best and she has your best interests at heart. I understand that it's hard for you to turn this part over, but it really is the best thing."

"I know in here," I pointed to my head.

An hour seemed like three. I was becoming antsier with every click of my watch. My palms were sweating, which could account for the four cups of caffeine I had in my system.

Finally I saw them coming toward us, sporting huge

smiles on their faces.

"What? What happened, I want every detail," I jumped them before they had a chance to sit down."

"They love you. One shop ordered twelve bags, ten prints, and fifty cards. They will order more as these sell, they don't have much storage space. The other store wants everything in late October for the Christmas season. They were very impressed and called you, 'fresh.'"

"I've always been fresh. I'm so excited, I can't stand it. New York for crying out loud."

"Don't get too excited too quick, it isn't always going to be this easy. A lot of the time people turn things down for various reasons, you can't take it personal." Veronica looked me in the eye.

She reached into her purse and laid a check on the table. "This is a ten percent deposit. I left a brochure and a card. I promised shipment on the day after we get home. We need to keep these people very happy."

I picked up the check, it was made out to Hope's Garden. My hands began to shake and my feet were bouncing like I had jumping beans in my blood.

"Now we have a history, we can now tell people in Seattle that you are being represented in New York," Burke was beaming.

Posy was uncharacteristically quiet until she finally said, "I feel like I've been to college."

Our steps were lighter as we walked north. We stopped at one of the vendors along the sidewalk and bought hot dogs with everything, including sauerkraut, on them. At Lindy's we had the famous strawberry cheesecake. Somewhere after our third soft pretzel with mustard, my stomach was begging me to leave it alone.

"Do we have to eat again, ever?" I asked in pain.

"Oh, I hope not. If no one minds, I'm going to change our dinner reservations to Monday night," Burke said.

That night we went to Radio City Music Hall and saw the amazing Rockettes. Back at the hotel, we fell into bed. I was asleep before I could undress.

As we stood outside of the hotel waiting to hail a cab we were surprised how few people were on the sidewalk on Sunday morning and that the street was void of traffic.

Standing across the street in front of Saint Patrick's Cathedral was a dream unfolding. The architecture took my breath away. The beige gray stone glistened in the sunlight as if imbedded with diamond flecks. Climbing the steps toward the entrance was humbling to the point of feeling myself shrink by the enormity of the church.

The large carved wood doors were a prelude to the magnificence inside. Burke opened one of the doors and the cool air overtook us as we entered the low-lit entrance. People were milling around and lighting votive candles that cast a red glow beside the wide altar. Some were in the pews praying, yet not a sound was heard. The silence was like a greeting from God. The enormous stain glass windows splashed color across the marble floor.

This was a place and experience I couldn't share. I didn't

want to follow anyone, converse with anyone, feel anyone next to me or look at the same thing someone else was seeing. I stood in front of Burke, Veronica and Posy, put my hand on my chest, pointed in the opposite direction and held up my other hand, indicating 'halt', then I turned and walked away.

Along the wall, behind the marble columns, I followed the small sculptured fourteen Stations of the Cross. My fingers lightly ran across the eleventh station, knowing that I probably shouldn't touch it.

I took a place in the back on the center isle. The church was full to capacity and those unable to sit stood shoulder to shoulder behind the pews.

As mass began, the alter boys came down the wide center isle, followed by the priests. They took their places on the opulent altar under the enormous crucifix.

I wasn't familiar with the protocol, being a Protestant. I didn't participate with the congregation. I sat, overwhelmed by the reverence that filled the sanctuary and was content just being there.

When mass was over, above and behind the sanctuary, a pipe organ began to fill the air with powerful resounding notes. It seemed to punctuate the service with an explanation point.

I stepped out before anyone else and stood off to the side of the open doors. The organ stopped and suddenly, above my head, tucked somewhere in the arch above the doors, baby birds were cheeping. Their tiny voices, a contrast to the large organ notes, were the sweetest sound. I looked out at the pavement and the brownstone buildings and wondered; where did the mama bird find worms to feed her kids?

People began to file out, Burke, Veronica, and Posy with them. They, like the rest were quiet, almost introspective.

We caught a cab to the Plaza Hotel for Sunday brunch. The cab driver was friendly and didn't honk his horn once the whole ride. The smell of exhaust of heavy traffic was gone. People strolled rather than sprinting along the sidewalks. Some had dogs on leashes, others held the hands of children and a few stopped at the newspaper stand to buy a thick Sunday edition and a cup of coffee. It was oddly serene.

The cab pulled under the marquee of the Plaza. Across the street to the entrance to Central Park, horses, attached to carriages, hung their heads in boredom.

The opulence of the lobby was matched only by the finely dressed people waiting for their place in line that led up the few steps to the upper level where the brunch was displayed and served.

If there was another way to prepare an egg, the chefs had not discovered it. Made to order omelets were being flipped in skillets over an open flame stove, eggs were poached, fried and soft boiled with the tops of the shell cut off. Massive amount of fruit was arranged as if in an old master painting. Pastry of every description, from Danish to cream puffs rested on silver platters. Bagels, muffins, crescent rolls and breads poked out from the tops of baskets. Thinly sliced lox and roast beef surrounded mountains of cracked crab. Bacon and little sausages were kept hot on the steam table. In the center of it all an ice sculpture glistened, surrounded by fresh flowers in crystal vases.

The mission to eat a little of everything required two hours of vigilance that produced misery.

We waddled across the street to walk off the pain in Central Park. We got as far as the first park bench. We sat there like whales needing to be re-released back into Puget Sound. Joggers ran past like gazelles.

"They say it takes four hours for food to digest. How much time is left?" I managed to mumble looking down at my protruding stomach that resembled a basketball.

Tomorrow we would get down to business, it was our last day and the time had come for Veronica and Posy to make their last calls. For now, we were exhausted and full of more than food. In our own unique way, each of us received gifts from The Big Apple this day.

When we could move once again we walked toward the hotel. We had most of the sidewalk to ourselves allowing us to look into the windows of the fine stores.

Taking a cab the rest of the way gave us a chance to rest and to digest the many flavors of the day. Sleep would come early and welcomed.

We were back on the sidewalk early the next morning thinking we would beat the traffic. Apparently everyone in the city had the same schedule, flowing in a continuous wave carrying paper cups full of coffee, waking up on the move.

The cab took us to Washington Square, the honking had returned as a necessary survival tool. The Monday frenzy had returned full force.

Washington Square on the other hand was tepid. We walked under the Washington Square North arch into the wide-open space that was sprinkled with a few young men playing guitars as a few couples milled about.

The shops and boutiques carried one of a kind fashions, designer jewelry, pottery and leather bags. The galleries varied in size as well as content and style. Veronica and Posy took notes on the places they wanted to call on.

While they were gone, Burke and I listened to the music and strolled around until we found a coffee shop.

"So, how are you doing with all of this?" Burke waved his hand in the air.

"It's overwhelming. I can't find the words to thank you Burke. You have turned my world upside down twice, I just—"

"No, wait, you have changed my life too. Without you I wouldn't have the woman of my dreams or the most fun I have ever had. Let's call it even steven. And Posy, well, she is just the icing on the cinnamon roll."

"It's all Veronica's fault. If she had been watching where she was going, she wouldn't have run into us."

We both laughed as he extended his hand and we shook on our mutual acknowledgment.

"We are building a future, all four of us."

"Yes, we are." I confirmed.

"Yes we are what?" Veronica asked, standing behind me.

"Building our future," Burke beamed when he saw her.

"Well?" I asked.

"It went ok. Some places said they would think about us, a couple of the managers weren't there and three ordered. They all liked your work. A gallery wants prints and cards, two boutiques want everything. We left brochures with five other places and I'm confident they will respond." Posy sounded like a pro already.

"Like a duck to water," Veronica smiled at her.

"Ok, it's time for lunch ladies," Burke said.

We walked back to Washington Square and caught a cab back to the deli close to our hotel.

Between bites of his corn beef sandwich Burke reminded us that we had reservations that night at one of the best Italian restaurants in the city. He told us about the marathon food fest; the antipasto tray, the bowls of minestrone soup, the bread and salad all before the entrée came.

"I have eaten more the past two days than I ate all last year, I would be happy with a cracker and a salad," I said.

"Thank you Hope." Veronica seemed relieved.

That night, for the last time, I laid on my bed and listened to the sounds of the traffic that had almost become a lullaby. I knew that I would have to come back someday to see the things that time had not allowed; the Metropolitan Museum of Art, which I was sure would take several days, the ferry boat ride around the Statue of Liberty and the Broadway shows.

We packed and took a cab to the airport. It had been a wondrous few days and another one of those life pivotal points.

I buckled my seat belt as the plane taxied toward the runway. The engines roared, the nose pulled up and we were in the air. Knowing what to expect erased the fear. The plane banked over the city as a farewell gesture. Looking out the window I thought, somewhere down there someone is pushing a shopping cart to nowhere and baby birds are learning to fly. I sighed and closed my eyes as we headed west.

We touched down at Sea-Tac airport just before sunset. After collecting our bags we stepped outside and took a deep breath of the sweet salt air. It was good to be home.

We recovered slowly from jet lag as we returned to our first order of business. While we were gone, Richard had the Hope's Garden sign installed over the door. It was the first thing we saw when we got off the bus.

"If you don't grab Richard while you have the chance, someone with good sense will," I said to Posy.

We instantly began to put together the orders to send to New York. I wrote a personal 'thank you' note to each one, enclosed it in the package and they were shipped that afternoon.

Veronica and Posy began to map out their territory, choosing to go to the tourist areas in and around the greater Seattle area and north. They would also search out Nurseries and garden shops.

I began to fine-tune my matting, trying to develop a rhythm and increase my speed.

We opened a Hope's Garden checking account and I wrote Burke his first check to put on his side of the ledger.

The orders dribbled in on a steady basis. New ones came in from the calls made in New York. I continued to come up with new designs. The framer came in twice a week. We were humming along.

With the increased responsibility I was forced to quit my job at the café. Trudy had been more than patient when I would call and ask to have a day off or to rearrange my hours. When I told her I had to donate full time to the business, she was sad but supportive.

"You have been a real beacon around here, we will always be friends. Go, do what you are meant to do. Just remember where the best cheeseburgers in town come from."

We gave each other a big hug. "I love you Trudy."

"Back atcha squirt."

On a Sunday afternoon, Posy and I walked down to the waterfront. It was a warm day and it was good to get some exercise.

"You have been quiet all day, is something bothering you?" Posy asked.

"Are you sick of riding the bus?"

"Never been my favorite thing."

"We need a car, nothing fancy, just a used something that runs."

"That would make carting things around easier, that's for sure."

"There's one more thing." I took a deep breath. "The contrast of all the room at work and the lack of space at home is getting to me. At home I'm feeling cramped and claustrophobic. When I worked at the café there wasn't such a difference. The studio also gives me a door to close when I need to concentrate."

"So what are you saying, exactly?"

"I would like for us to check into renting a house, but I seriously think we need a car mostly right now. What do you think? Our world is expanding and we can't move around in it."

"It would be nice to go to the store and buy more than two bags of groceries. It would give us freedom, that's for sure. Can we afford it though?"

"I don't know, it depends. Let's just find out what's out there and how much it costs. At least we will know then. If we find something, Richard can look it over to see if it's ok, he knows about those things."

"Do you have a driver's license?" She asked.

"Yes, but it will have to be changed to a Washington license. Do you?'

"Yeah"

When we returned home we took the coffee can out of the refrigerator and dumped out the savings money on the bed. We counted out six hundred dollars.

"Well," I said. "At least we know what the bottom line is."

"It scares me to spend our savings." Posy frowned.

"I know, but a person has to take a leap of faith sometimes. I guess we should know that better than most people."

We searched the paper everyday for a couple of weeks.

Every car was out of our price range. The pile of newspapers was growing, as was our frustration. Then we saw the most unusual add that said in big bold type; 'Home Wanted." We read farther; 'Moving to Europe, must sell to the buyer of our choice, 1972 Family Friend, excellent condition, will discuss price, all calls screened.'

I called the number and told the man who I was and why I was calling. I explained our situation as briefly as possible, leaving out the part about being homeless at one time. He said that he had bought the car as a wedding present for his wife and she loved the car. He had received a job offer, too good to refuse, in London and couldn't take the car with them. He didn't want to sell the car to someone that wouldn't take care of it. He said to think of it more like an adoption and he laughed. I invited him and his wife to come to the studio to meet us and to see that we were legitimate. We made an appointment for the following morning.

I called Burke and Veronica to see if they could be at the studio at ten o'clock in the morning to add their support.

Burke and Veronica were there when we arrived at nine. We had coffee in the lunchroom and discussed the situation.

"Try to be charming, I'm trying to impress these people," I chided Burke.

They arrived right on time. We gave them a tour of the studio, with Burke as tour guide. He told them that he had another business, but had so much faith in Posy and me that he couldn't resist the opportunity to work with us. Veronica told them about our customers in New York and our future plans.

They were very interested. Mark, the man, said he would like to take some brochures to London with him in case he saw a possibility arise there.

They took us down the street where the car was parked. It was red, shiny and without a scratch or dent.

"There it is, isn't it beautiful?" Linda pointed to her prize.

"Beautiful it is," Posy said.

We asked Richard to come out and take a look. He joined us, walked around the car and said, "What a beauty, can you pop the hood for me?"

He looked at the engine, listened to it, checked the underside and emerged with a big smile.

Back in the studio we discussed price. They wanted six hundred fifty and we offered six hundred. They agreed, reluctantly.

"As soon as we find the house we are looking to rent we will make sure she has a garage to live in," I said.

"In the mean time she can sleep in my garage," Veronica said, laughing.

"Did you see our add under 'house for rent?"

"What?" Posy asked

"We are looking for someone to rent our house for two years. My company is opening an office in London and I have been given the position of Vice President. We are going to give it a try to see if we like it before we make a commitment. We want someone in the house that we trust will take care of it and maintain the yard. We are going to store our personal things, but will leave a lot of the furniture and the appliances in the house. My brother is available in case of an emergency but he can't be there all the time. If you are interested, come see the place. I think we can work something out," the man said.

"Where are you located?" Veronica asked.

"The Greenlake area," he said.

"I can take you," Veronica offered, looking at Posy and me.

"Sure, that's fine with me if it's ok with them."

"Fine with us," I said.

"Excellent," he smiled and gave us directions.

We drove north along the East Side of the lake. Just past the lake we found the address. It was an older, classic, well-manicured neighborhood. Mature Japanese Elms and shrubbery framed the house. The flowerbeds were weed less and in full spring bloom. We rang the doorbell and Mark answered with a friendly smile as he checked the Cadillac parked at his curb. "Welcome, come in."

The front room greeted us with a warm glow coming from the large bay windows. The wood floors gleamed under the Persian rugs. The furniture was in the cozy traditional style.

"Let us show you around," Linda said.

The dining room was small but comfortable. The kitchen, with white cabinets, was light and cheerful with a breakfast nook with pale yellow walls. A white, glass top, wrought iron table with yellow tulips in the center was inviting. A small den was off the kitchen and down the hall a bathroom, also in white and yellow. Three bedrooms and bathroom were up the wood stairs. The laundry room was in the basement.

Mark explained, "We are going to store the antique furniture, the grandfather clock, dishes, beds and odds and ends. Does anyone have any questions?"

"Are you storing your lawn mower?" Posy asked.

"Not necessarily."

"What do you want for rent?"

"Well, like I said, we basically want to have the house lived in and maintained. It isn't so much about the money. We still own the house so we have to pay the insurance and the taxes. We were thinking five hundred a month, which will cover our storage cost. The rent would be sent directly to our bank in Seattle.

"Can we have a moment?" Veronica asked.

"Sure, take your time," he said walking into the kitchen.

"Before you freak out completely, you need to listen to me. I write the checks for B.T. Development, I know how much your salary is. You each make twelve thousand dollars a year, that's a thousand dollars a month. If the utilities are a hundred fifty a month, you're each paying two hundred fifty a month, which leaves you seven fifty a month left over. Trust me, there is nothing out there that can touch the quality for the cost."

We didn't say anything until she called Mark and Linda to come back into the room.

"I just want you to know up front that we don't drink,

smoke or do drugs. We don't have wild parties and we love flowers, obviously," I said.

"I might have a boyfriend soon, I haven't made up my mind yet. You met him this morning, he owns the bicycle shop next to the studio. He is very handy with things, so if anything breaks, we won't have to bother your brother."

"He is quite adorable," Linda smiled.

"I knew you were quality people this morning. I appreciate your candor."

"When do you have to be in London?" Veronica asked.

"In a month."

I nodded my head. "That works for us. Can we pick up the car in three weeks? That way, we will have a way to move and it can stay in the garage in the mean time."

"Sure, we will have things in order by then and the papers drawn up as well," Mark said.

We shook hands, thanked them and drove back along the lake. Posy shouted, 'Look' pointing to the bicycle riders on the cement path that goes around the lake.

"What have we just done?" I felt a freak out moment coming on.

"Something down right fantastic," Veronica slapped the dashboard.

"Easy for you to say."

"I have a place to ride my bike without being killed," Posy squealed.

Burke splashed Bay Rum on his clean-shaven face, ran a

comb through his wet wavy hair and went into the kitchen to see his wife standing over the stove.

"What smells like French toast?" he said lovingly.

"French toast. I thought it might be nice to have breakfast outside," she smiled.

"That would be very nice, what can I do?"

"Take these plates out, I'll be right there."

The table was set, the coffee was hot and the orange juice was cold. She had picked roses from one of her bushes and placed them in a glass bowl for the center of the table. He thought of his long demised plant and smiled.

They sat across from each other. "I wonder if Denny's misses me?" he said.

After breakfast they went to Burke's place to finish clearing out the rest of his things from his townhouse before calling the Realtor to put it on the market.

Veronica stood in the middle of his front room giving her a panoramic view.

"Burke, are you attached to anything?" she asked in amazement at his austere life style. There wasn't a picture anywhere on the walls, not one book rested on an end table. She was surprised that she had never given it much thought on the few times she had been there.

"I'm attached to you."

"That's sweet, but I mean stuff wise, are you attached to any object?"

"Not much, objects are just that."

"Do you own a vacuum cleaner?"

"No, the lady that cleans owns a vacuum cleaner."

"That would be me from now on. Is the vase that we bought on our honeymoon just an object?"

"No, that's a prized possession."

"Why?"

"Because, it has love all over it, whenever I look at it, I remember us."

Close to tears from being the cause of him having something he highly valued and because he had so few attachments, she turned away and distracted herself by unfolding boxes.

Soon he was beside her. "Know what I would really like to have?"

"What?"

"A camera. We don't have any pictures of our romance, like the ferry ride. I wish I had pictures of you feeding the gulls, that was such a precious sight. We don't have pictures of Alice, or our honeymoon. Why don't either one of us have a camera?"

She began to sob. She didn't realize how much these moments had mattered to him.

"Oh honey, I'm sorry. What did I say?"

"Nothing, really. I just didn't know that you were so sentimental."

"I wasn't, it's an acquired skill. I wanted to record things all of a sudden. No, all of a sudden I have things to record and save."

Veronica went into his bedroom and the tears instantly became laughter when she saw the red and blue plaid sheets on his rumpled unmade bed.

"What?" He poked his head in the door.

"I can't believe these sheets," she said, still laughing.

"Veronica, do not laugh at my decorating expertise."

"Which part isn't funny, decorating or expertise?"

He laughed with her then turned serious, "You are looking at a moment in history. That's the way those sheets were left when I jumped out of them the day I married you."

"Are you attached to those sheets Burke?"

"Well, yeah, I am actually."

"Ok, they go home with us then"

"I don't know what to do with all this furniture."

"We could make a den in the basement."

"You have a basement?"

"Yes, WE have a basement. You could have your own space down there. What do you think about giving the girls the bedroom set? They are one short on beds?"

"That would be great. The movers could take it to them before they deliver the rest of the furniture. Thanks for the thought, somehow it doesn't seem to fit anywhere."

They packed the rest of the few boxes and cleared out his closet. It was now official.

After hanging his clothes in her closet they stepped back and looked.'

"Doesn't that look friendly?" Veronica beamed.

"Yes dear, it sure does."

With Posy and Veronica on a road trip to Astoria and Seaside, Oregon I took the four days to bury myself in work.

Thinking about the car and the house only divided my attention and made the time drag.

I needed some new designs for a revised catalog and began to work on ideas that had been building in my mind. The once tidy drawing table was now an organized chaos of paper scattered across the top and pens thrown about at will.

I decided to spend the nights at the studio to give me more working time and to avoid taking the bus.

One evening Richard came in looking like a man that just lost his puppy.

"Hi Richard, what's going on?"

"Nothing, that's the problem. I brought a pizza, could you have dinner with me? I need a friend."

"I suppose, I can't take long though, I'm swamped to the gills."

We sat in the lunchroom, he was visibly distraught. "I don't know what to do about Posy. I really like her but she has such high walls around her I can't seem to get through. Why doesn't she just tell me if she doesn't like me?"

"I don't think she doesn't like you."

"Then what is it? I'm not real good at figuring these things out, I don't read minds well. I don't mean to pry, but has she said anything about me?"

"I don't know what's going on. She likes you, but won't talk about you. Trust me, I have pleaded your case, but she just clams up. I have no advice for you because I honestly don't know where she's coming from in her mind."

"What's her story anyway?"

"I don't know. We are friends, roommates, and are in business together. She made it clear when we met that the past is the past and she lives in the moment. She will open up a little from time to time, on her terms. I respect that and don't push her. This I do know, she is the kindest person I know, she is honest and I trust her."

"What's wrong with a crummy lunch for crying out loud? It's just sharing a sandwich, I'm not asking her to marry me."

"I don't know Richard, just hang in there until you don't think it's worth it any more. No one can tell you, you're the only one that can know that."

"Ok" he said, putting the pizza box in the trash. "Thanks, you helped, sorta."

Veronica and Posy came back with orders from Seaside. There would be a big turn over with the tourist season in full swing.

Three weeks went by quickly. All of a sudden the day before Mark and Linda were to bring the car was upon us. We couldn't contain our excitement when we bought the cashiers check for six hundred dollars. We had put our coffee can money into a savings account to draw interest and took the car money out of our checking account.

We had our updated driver's licenses and the check when they arrived the next morning. Linda wasn't smiling. Mark had the title with our names on it and had transferred the insurance into our names.

"Don't go out to the car until we are gone," Linda said handing us an envelope with the papers and key inside.

"Please know that we are going to take very special care of the car," I said trying to reassure her.

"I'm selling my wedding present," she said, looking down at the floor.

Veronica gave her a hug, "I just got married, so I know how hard this must be for you."

"Thanks." And they walked out the door.

Despite being anxious, we waited a respectable amount of time before we went down to the street to find our car. We just stood looking at it for a while.

We flipped a coin and Posy won the right to be the first driver. We sat in the seats looking at the interior and feeling the fabric of the seats.

"Yahoo," Posy yelled turning the key. She drove several blocks, far too cautiously.

"Posy, someone is going to run into us if you don't at least keep up with the traffic."

"Fine, you drive, I'm too nervous."

I pulled up close to the studio and tried four times to parallel park until the car in front of the space pulled out. Clearly, we had some work to do.

"How did it go?" Burke asked.

"Fine, except for the parking part."

"You can park behind the building beside the Dumpster in the alley."

"I thought that was just for you."

"It's for anyone that works here. You can make the car go forward and backward, right?" Burke laughed.

"Don't be a smart alec, it's going sideways that's the problem. Where I come from people park nose first."

Despite our doubts that it would ever happen, moving day did arrive. Trudy and Larry brought their pick-up, loaded it with our bed, furniture and our few boxes looking like the Beverly Hillbillies. We drove off with the pick-up following us. There was a bittersweet ache in our heart. We had been happy in the apartment, but at the same time we were looking forward to being in the house and to all that was to come.

We parked in front of the house with Trudy and Larry behind us. We all stood on the sidewalk watching the sprinkler make little rainbows above the newly mowed lawn. How ironic, I thought, they are leaving and Mark is watering the grass.

We rang the doorbell. Linda opened the door and called to Mark. Their luggage was lined up in the entry.

"How are you?" Mark said in a somber tone.

Linda started walking through the house, crying more with every room. It was a very awkward moment. My excitement splattered at my feet on the tile entry, knowing this home belonged to a lady with a breaking heart.

"We are spending the night close to the airport, we have an early flight in the morning. Here's the key and you need to sign the agreement papers," Mark said.

We signed and I looked up at him, "We will take care of everything Mark. Your brother is welcome to drop by at anytime without notice."

"I know, this is just hard. Don't forget to turn off the

hose."

Linda came back into the room and took his arm, "We have to go now."

They walked out the door without looking back. Linda must have called a cab because there was one parked in front of Linda's car. My heart sank watching her gently touch it as she passed it to get into the cab.

I sat down on the yellow couch that didn't fit my body yet. Posy sat in a wing back chair. Trudy and Larry walked through the house. A heavy cloud obscured the sun coming through the windows.

We were quiet until the doorbell rang. The movers had arrived with Burke's bedroom furniture.

"Where do you want this?" The big burly man wanted to know.

"Let me find out, I'll be right back."

Posy and I went upstairs and picked our rooms. The bedrooms were empty, we made our choice. We split the furniture, Posy took the bed, dresser and one night stand. I took the old bed, chest of drawers and the other night stand.

After the pick-up was unloaded, Trudy came to the rescue in her typical direct way. "Ok you two, take ten minutes, then enjoy this opportunity. Those people will be fine as soon as they get there. They have a wonderful adventure ahead of them. No one can move forward unless someone else makes a shift."

"We want to invite you to dinner some Sunday soon."

"We'll look forward to it," Larry said as they walked out.

We began to unpack right away. We made our beds and put the essentials in spaces where we could find them. We went out for sandwiches and drove around to get familiar with the area. Shopping was within a close distance and to our surprise, the zoo was close by.

I found myself rolling over in my sleep that night, taking up the whole bed. As the sunlight came through the windows I woke up slowly, enjoying the delicious moment of waking up alone with no need to rush.

I looked out the window over the kitchen sink and watched Posy walking around the fenced back yard, taking her own moment. She pulled the only weed on the property. Our new life had begun, again.

One Saturday morning we decided to try a new supermarket. When we parked the car and walked toward the strip mall we saw a pet store.

Posy pointed to the sign, *Perfect Pal Pets*. "Let's go in and look at the birds. Maybe they have a little Malcolm."

We walked into a menagerie of feathers, fur and fins. We looked at the parakeets, finches, and doves. We watched the beautiful saltwater fish swim in miniature oceans.

The puppies sparked our attention but not our checkbook. Each puppy was a pure bred with a price tag to match.

After shopping we drove through an unfamiliar area of our neighborhood, so we didn't realize that the animal shelter was close by. I hit the brake and squealed into the parking lot. We were on a mission. Go look. Get the warm fuzzy out of our system and move on. The walk down the aisle with cages on each side was heart wrenching. Every size, color, and breed of canine yelped and jumped for favored consideration. I didn't make eye contact.

We saw a cage on the floor level that seemed empty. I got down on my hands and knees to look inside. Huddled in the back corner a small Pomeranian trembled, looking out at me with pitiful eyes.

"We think he has been abused," the attendant said sadly.

Posy was sitting in front of the cage. "He's the one."

The attendant unlatched the cage, reached in and pulled out a handful of disheveled fluff.

I took the little thing out of his hands and held the shaking body close to my neck. I began to hum softly. He licked my ears and was still. I handed him to Posy. He licked her nose. It was over. Our hearts were taken.

On the way home he fell asleep in Posy's lap as she continued to stroke his head.

We put him in the backyard right away. The moment his nickel-size paws made contact with the lawn; he catapulted across the yard to the back flower garden marking every bush and then he ran in circles; leaped into the air almost turning somersaults. He barked and looked at us as if to say, "See how special I am." We named him Apollo.

Two months passed. The business was growing. Veronica and Posy made calls three days a week. Veronica worked at B.T. Development the other two days while Posy worked in her office writing orders, setting up accounts and answering phone calls. On weekends we turned to our domestic side with yard work and household chores.

Richard and Posy were at least having lunch once in awhile. They rode their bikes around the lake from time to time. Once he stayed for dinner and a game of scrabble. Their friendship was growing, enough for him to think it was still worth it.

Posy was beginning to enjoy his company and his quirky sense of humor that matched hers. He made her laugh.

Still she was reluctant to be vulnerable. Any attempt of affection on his part was shunned in a most subtle way.

PART FOUR

It had been an unusually challenging day of telephone tag. I have a vile disgust for answering machines, except my own. All day I had no human contact, only leaving my voice going out into the atmosphere after the beep.

It seemed that the pages of the calendar had been torn off in a flurry. I was suddenly writing deadlines in September's squares. It was still warm and Christmas orders were coming in at a full gallop.

I thought Veronica was picking Posy up at the house and that they were coming back to the studio in the afternoon. I was further behind than when I started.

Exhausted from the race to nowhere and frustrated, I shoved myself to get through traffic, assuming Veronica had been delayed somewhere.

Apollo greeted me at the door. All he required was a pat on the head and the privilege of following me everywhere.

"How's life in the puppy world?"

The house was creepy in its stillness. I began to shiver. There was only one light on in the den. I turned on more lamps and went into the kitchen. The dishes had been washed and were on a towel on the counter. Braced against the coffeepot was a note in Posy's handwriting; "I don't expect you to understand. I have a journey to take, I don't know how long I will be gone." That was it, cold and to the point yet saying nothing at all.

In one second the world became flash frozen in time. I called Veronica at BT, she had left moments ago. I called the house and got their answering machine leaving a brief frantic message. I called Richard, there was no answer.

Within a half an hour Veronica called. "What do you mean she's gone?"

"She left a note, I thought she was with you all day, have you seen her?"

"No, she called me this morning saying she wouldn't be able to make calls today. I thought she was going to the studio to work. What does the note say?"

I read it to her, my voice and hands shaking.

"Burke is motioning to me, we are coming over." She hung up the phone before I could respond.

I plugged in the coffee, fed the dog and sat on the floor in the kitchen. My head was full of fuzz. Apollo came over and licked my face. I picked him up and put him in my lap.

Within an hour I heard Veronica and Burke open the front door. I got up and called them into the kitchen. I poured coffee and we sat down at the table. I handed Burke the note.

"I don't get it. Has she been upset or anything, why do you think she did this?"

"I don't have a clue. Should we call the police and file a

missing persons report?" I had to do something.

"I don't think it will do any good. Technically, she isn't missing because she left a note. They will probably say she left on her own free will."

"Great! I'm really mad right now."

"What can we do to help?"

"I have been on the phone all day trying to answer questions that belong to Posy. I don't know what delivery dates she has given to people, or whether their accounts have been set up. I have left messages to the whole world. Veronica, if you could try to sort this out in the morning, I'll be in as soon as I can."

"Sure, I'll go through the invoices and get on the phone. Anything else?"

"No, I'll keep trying to get hold of Richard, maybe he has some ideas. I really appreciate you coming over but I just need to be alone right now."

"We understand, try not to worry too much."

I tried Richard's number again, "Hello," he said.

"Richard, this is Hope. Have you seen Posy today?"

"No, we were going to have lunch but she didn't show up. I figured I'd been ditched or she got tied up somewhere, why?"

"She's gone." I read him the note.

"That doesn't make sense," he said obviously upset.

"Did you guys have a fight or something?"

"No, nothing at all. This is too weird."

"Do you think I should call the police?"

"They aren't going to do anything, she left a note, so she isn't missing. They have robbers and murderers to catch. This isn't even a blip on their radar screen. If you hear anything from her at all, please call me right away and I'll do the same."

"Ok, good night for now."

I curled up on the couch, wrapping myself in a blanket. My next awareness was the dim light easing through the bay windows. I had no recall of the night passing.

I didn't remember making the morning coffee, but I heard the pot click on. I got up, filled my mug and went upstairs like a robot. I was moving, but there was no feeling, only numbness in every step. I set the shower to scalding and sat on the floor letting the water pelt my face until the tank ran cold.

As I wrapped my terry cloth robe around me I saw the old hotel towel in the frame on the wall. It had been one of our first decorating projects when we moved into the house.

Somewhere in the distance I heard a scream as I picked up a bar of soap and threw it at the glass, shattering it all over the floor. Without knowing it I cut my feet and tracked blood down the hall and into my bedroom leaving red footprints on the off white carpet.

I went into her room and opened her closet doors. Everything was there, hanging neatly on satin hangers. It looked like some jeans and shirts were missing with several pair of shoes.

The phone rang while I was trying to blot up the carpet. I almost tripped to get it before the machine clicked on.

"Hello."

"Hope, are you coming in today?" Veronica sounded concerned.

"No, I seem to be going from rack to ruin, I would only do more damage than good."

"Don't worry, I was only asking? We have it covered."

I put my brain on rewind. What was I missing? Was there a sign I didn't see? Where had she been all this time? She seemed happy, I just didn't get it.

Out of the blue, without warning I was hit with a panic attack. Was I broke? We had maintained our financial arrangement. Mine was mine, hers was hers and ours was ours. Ours, however was the household account. I called the bank, had there been any cash withdrawals in the past few days? No, the account had not been touched. I told them that from this moment on I was the only one authorized to write checks on that account, explaining lightly the situation, without going into detail.

I roamed the house looking at the stuff that we knew had to live here. I picked up that awful ceramic bunny and laughed in spite of myself. I loved that bunny.

I tried to sleep but only took a series of naps. I wasn't interested in food. The day blended with the night and I had no concept of time.

When I awoke at six the next morning, the pain hit me like an ice storm. My feet hit the floor and I went through the routine and went to the studio like a zombie.

Burke was in the lunchroom with Veronica when I arrived. I sat down with them and we tried to figure out where to go next.

"Someone is going to have to take up Posy's slack," Burke said.

"Who has enough slack of their own to take up hers?"

"I don't know, but somehow we are not going to let our customers down, no matter what."

"Then we don't add any new accounts until we are able to service the ones we have now. I don't think we should hire someone new right now, they would have to be trained and that takes time. She couldn't have left at a worse time." I was becoming angrier by the moment.

"Well, we'll just have to think of something," Burke sighed

The line at the check in counter was long and impatient. People shoved luggage at each other. Unattended children ran amuck. Parents, unable to forfeit their places in line to reel them in could only scream at them with no results. Numb and oblivious, Posy could only move forward as she was nudged from behind.

In some surreal dream she moved with the mass toward the gate. Seated and buckled, she put on the earphones, a subliminal 'Do Not Disturb' sign. The seats next to her were empty and she was grateful.

The engines roared and the ground dropped away. She looked out the window and watched Puget Sound become a pond. Weary she closed her eyes. Too many nights without sleep had taken their toll. She had drifted through the darkness trying to balance the nagging pain on the inside with the wonder of her life on the outside. She thought it would pass or at least she could endure, but the hurt of unfinished business and questions had won out. She had wrestled too long, she wanted to have her life homogenized somehow. Living in the moment wasn't working anymore.

Painfully she remembered that hot July day that was a pivotal moment in her life. She had been sitting on the front porch with her mother drinking lemonade.

"I have to get away for awhile, I'm stuck in the mud here," she had said.

"You have responsibilities, you can't just take off."

"Just for a while, Mama."

The next day she packed her car and kissed her mother. Her dad was in the barn and didn't come out when she drove down the dusty road to the highway.

She arrived in Seattle not knowing what she was looking for and with little money. She hadn't been prepared for how much it would cost for food and gas.

She remembered that she hadn't told Hope the whole story when she had asked about Auntie Bea. There is an old saying where she grew up, 'the less said the better.' So she had skimmed over the highlights and let it go at that.

Not knowing where to go in a city larger than she had imagined, she drove the downtown streets toward the water. The hills and the traffic scared her to death. She had never seen the likes of either one of them before.

Wanting to save as much money as possible, she discovered the area around the docks and waterfront provided parking space and fish bars for inexpensive food. There were also public rest rooms with hot water in the sinks.

She slept in her car, thankful it was summer and warm. Every day she would move to another parking space thinking it would make it harder for her to be noticed.

One night she was dozing when she heard a pounding on the driver's window. Startled and terrified, she opened her eyes and saw a young man's face pressed to the glass. He smiled and she trembled. He motioned for her to roll down the window. He was either a cop or a killer, she had thought. She rolled down the window to a thin crack, just enough to hear his voice.

"What do you want?" She could hardly speak.

"Are you nuts or what? Don't you know it's dangerous down here? That Nebraska license plate is a red flag for trouble."

"Are you going to hurt me? I don't have any money."

"No, I'm not going to hurt you, I'm trying to save you. Around here, you need friends. I've seen your car for days, night and day."

"I'm not selling."

"Do I look like a pimp to you?"

"I don't know, I've never seen one before. I don't want drugs."

"I'm not a drug dealer either. Look, I hang out over there." He pointed to the viaduct. "It's safe there, no one will hurt you. You'll be welcome. You can come now or in the morning, it's up to you."

"Maybe in the morning, who do I ask for?"

"Flash, just Flash." He turned and walked away.

With the first light she woke up cold and hungry. There was no direction for her, she felt lost and alone. She walked toward the viaduct. People were standing around talking, some were waiting for the small fire to boil coffee. Others slept like lumps against the far wall. She stood like a statue outside the periphery, not daring to set one foot over the invisible line into a world she had never seen.

Turning around to leave she heard a voice yelling, "Hey, wait!" She turned and saw Flash running toward her. When he got to her, he grabbed her arm.

She jerked her arm back screaming, "Don't touch me."

"Sorry," he said and stepped away from her.

Suddenly a large imposing woman was standing beside him. "Leave her alone. Can't you see she's scared?"

"She's from Nebraska of all places. She needs help, she's been wandering around for days. I was just trying to keep her here before something happens to her."

"They call me Auntie Bea. If you're fond of drink or drugs there's no place for you here."

"That's not my style," she had said.

"Well then, if there is anything you want to know about this place, I'm the one to ask. If you need someone to talk to I'm the one to see. We have little but we share. Face it child, we all got here somehow."

She had put a "For Sale" sign in the rear window of the

car and within a few days there was a phone number under her windshield wiper. In a few days more she had two hundred fifty dollars in her jeans and a boulder removed from her shoulders.

The stewardess brought her back to reality, trying to initiate a conversation, "Can I get you anything? How are you doing?"

"Just spiffy, thank you. No, I don't care for anything right now." She put the earphones on again.

Before she knew it, they were over the Rocky Mountains. She looked out the window at the white, craggy tops of the Continental Divide. She closed her eyes as the plane's nose pointed straight down. There was no gradual descent into Denver, it was over the mountains and directly down. Her ears began to pop.

The wheels squeaked, the engines reversed and the plane eased its way to the gate of the airport. She collected her baggage, rented a car and pointed her way East.

Out of the city at last, she took a deep breath. The road was long, flat and void of traffic, she was off the interstate highway where few people traveled. She knew the road well. Fields of tall green corn created a patchwork across the flat landscape. Occasionally stately poplar and aged oak trees broke the space between the monotonous horizon line. Sometimes a red barn splashed a defiant color on the landscape; a survivor, strong and resilient. Black Angus polka dots on green, grazed without ceasing. The sweet mundane slowly eased through her like a glowing lava lamp.

She slowed the car, looking for a place to pull over. Dirt farm roads dissected the highway. She stopped, got out of the car and stretched out her arms, knowing if they were long enough, she could reach for miles without touching anything. A rabbit leaped across the road. She took off her shoes and dug her toes into the warm, dry, sandy soil. The earth hugged her feet like it did when they were much smaller. She lifted her leg and watched the dirt fall from her foot, her roots exposed. She wiggled her toes, "This little piggy ran home," she thought.

She threw her shoes into the back seat and turned the key. She looked up at the white puffy clouds that reminded her of the cotton candy when the carnival had come to town. She turned on the radio and continued to eat up the familiar miles; much like having leftovers.

The sun reluctantly hung on the curve of the earth behind her, turning an orange, vermilion and pink splash across the hot summer sky.

Her heart began to pound when she made the turn down the oak-lined road. Her dad's old boots turned upside down on the fence posts were like old friends. She pulled into the yard, took a deep breath and got out of the car. The front door was open, lights were on in the front room, but no one was home. She opened the screen door and looked inside. Nothing had changed. Every picture hung in the same place on the ever-white walls. The big soft couches still sported the afghans on their backs. There was something eerie about how the clocks hadn't seemed to tick away the years.

She closed the screen door and stood for a while on the front porch listening to the crickets. The horses in the pasture grazed lazily. Hollyhocks in bloom by the front door stood tall and in full bloom reminding her of the hollyhock dolls she made when she was a child.

Disappointed, she got back in the car and drove to town hoping to find them. The drug store was open. She sat down at the counter and ordered a cup of coffee. Old man Hunter looked at her with a frown, and then broke into a laugh, "Well, I'll be darned, it's you. Where have you been?"

"Out west. Do you know where the folks might be?"

"Well, they might be at the neighbors, I'll call and see." She listened to him on the phone; 'No, I'm not kidding. Hold on, I'll put her on.' He handed me the receiver.

"Hello." All she heard was sobbing on the other end.

"Mama? Mama, stop crying. I'll meet you at home."

She drove back to the farm. Twilight was turning the barn, house and outbuildings into silhouettes. As she drove down the road she saw headlights coming toward her across the pasture that separated their place from the Russell's.

Their car screeched to a stop, car doors flew open and her mother ran toward her, almost knocking her down with the momentum. They hugged. They cried and hugged again. Her dad stood back not wanting to come between them and not knowing what to do.

Posy looked past her mother at the mountain of a man, imposing by his height. Peeking around the back of his leg, a little boy said shyly, "Do we have company, daddy?"

"Yes, we have company, son."

Posy looked at the beautiful child; blond curly hair, freckles on his tan cheeks and eyes the color of topaz.

"He's grown," was all she could say.

"What do you expect after all," her father said coldly.

"Don't start," her mother warned as she blew her nose. "Let's be nice to each other Ralph,"

The boy braved the moment and stood in front of Posy, "Do I know you?"

"No, I don't think so." She choked.

Her mother motioned toward the house. "Come in. Are you hungry, dear? We have chicken and gooseberry pie in the fridge."

"Thanks, Mama."

They spent the evening in polite chit-chat avoiding speaking of everything of any meaning. She learned who got married, who got divorced; about the drop in beef prices and the sugar beets. The irrigation ditches were drying up from lack of rain and the pastures were straw. The river was down. Farmers were selling out from lack of moisture and ranchers were forced to buy feed at an outrageous price.

At last her father looked at the boy behind the funny papers, "Time for you to go to bed now, son."

"Do I have to?"

"When I say it's bedtime, it's bedtime."

He put Dick Tracy into the magazine rack. "Good night Mama, good night Daddy." He kissed them both and went to his room in the basement.

Posy yawned, "I think I'll turn in too. It's been a long day."

"Sleep well dear," her mother said. Her father didn't say anything.

She turned on the light in her room and was shocked. She felt twelve again. Her stuffed animals, friendly and fuzzy were still waiting on her bed covered with the quilt that had always been there. Her books and pictures of high school friends had not been moved. She looked at the pictures, remembering the time and event when each was taken. She laughed at the moment and at how young they looked. There in an 8x10 frame a young man grinned at her. She picked it up and looked into his eyes, the glacier-blue eyes that could turn her heart to mush. In the bottom corner he had signed, "I will always love you—Dustin." She touched his nose, turned out the light and crawled under the quilt. She was exhausted.

Her body slowly sank into the mattress. She pulled the quilt up over her head and waited, waited for the sound she knew would come. Then there it was, right on time. Across the Platte river the CB&Q hugged the tracks, slowed down and blew its whistle; two long and one short, repeated three times as the train was going through town.

As she did when she was a child; she wondered where it was going and where it came from. The engineer probably didn't hook the mail or pick up the milk cans anymore but the sound was the same. The sounds of a train in the night, as well as cellos and harmonicas, could pierce her heart to the core and make her cry from a sadness that she didn't understand.

She awoke to the heavy smell of hickory-smoked bacon and rich coffee. She lay still for a while, sinking into the feather bed.

She looked around the room. Dustin was still smiling. She wondered why she didn't feel sadness or longing or anything at all. He had been her best friend; they had gone steady; he had given her his high school ring that she had worn on a gold chain around her neck, but had she loved him? He had been kind to her, respectful and loving. Her parents liked him, every one did. He had an easy way about him, was charming with stunning good looks.

Sometimes she had felt like a bird with clipped wings. His love was too big, too perfect. They were young and the world to her was too inviting. At night she would listen to the distant trains going to far off places and she would feel an ache in her heart. During the day she would look at the horizon and try to imagine what was on the other side.

Dustin had been clear on how he wanted his life to be; marry her, have kids, own a business and play his music. Those were his heart's desire. She, on the other hand, didn't have a clue. What she did know for sure was that somewhere over that flat horizon was a magnet pulling at her.

She sighed and slowly got out of the warm bed. In the kitchen her parents were playing a game of cribbage.

"Who's winning?"

"He is, but he cheats," her mother smiled.

"He's still cheating? I'm going to walk around a little."

She poured a cup of coffee.

Outside, a dry sun promised a scorching day. She walked down the slope and into the cool dark barn. 'Unbelievable' she said to herself aloud. There was a whole life in there. Nothing had been thrown away. Saddles in every size and condition, bridles, hackamores and halters hung on hooks. Her dad's old chaps with the holes in the knees bore the wear and tear of many brandings and round-ups.

The smell of leather, tractor oil, hay and forty years of milking cows, birthing calves and foals all seemed to seep from the rough walls and hang in the air. The worn faded Wrangler jacket with its fringed cuffs was casually thrown across the top of the milk separator. Remembering the smell of that separator being cleaned with boiling water almost turned her stomach again. To this day she could hardly look at cottage cheese. Tears came to her eyes when she saw the milking stool that brought so much grief to her young life. She remembered that she never did get the hang of milking and was always the last one to let her heifers out the old wood door. She hated those cows and the feeling had been mutual. They would swish their smelly tails in her face and despite the hobbles, tried to kick the bucket she pressed between her knees.

A small silhouette in the barn door caught her attention.

"Whatcha doin? Daddy made pancakes and it ain't even Sunday or my birthday."

"You're a fine looking fellow, very grown up. So when's your birthday?"

"Not for a long time, next week. I have my own calf,

I saw her being born, it was gross. After we have pancake bunnies, I'll show her to ya. I have to feed her milk from the bucket. Daddy calls it weaning, but she just sticks her head in the bucket, throws her head back and spills milk all over the place. It makes me mad cause I can't hold the bucket down. Do you want to help me feed the chickens? Daddy won't let me go up in the hayloft, says it's dangerous and the swallows might get me."

"That's quite a mouthful to chew for such a young man. How about we go up to the house and we'll deal with all of that later, ok?"

"Ok, come on, hurry, the pancakes are getting cold."

There wasn't much said at the table apart from the occasional, "close your mouth when you chew, son" and "looks like another day without rain".

After the plates were empty and the coffeepot had been drained, her dad ruffled the boy's hair and said, "Let's go see if we can get that old John Deere running. Probably have to go to town for new spark plugs."

"And Popsicles, daddy?"

"Well, you betcha." He said with a grin.

She watched her mother standing at the sink. Her back was slightly stooped from too much weight on her shoulders.

"You can't take it back, you know." Her mother said, not turning around.

"What?"

"The years. The first tooth, the first step, measles, smiles, Santa Claus. The pain the first time the school bus drives up the road. The first time only happens once."

"You never saw it from my side did you?"

"No, no, I only saw it from his side. While you and Dustin were following your separate young dreams, he got stuck with old parents."

She put down the sponge, turned and looked at her daughter. "I look at him and see the little girl that lit up my life the moment she came out of my body. In that instant I felt love, the kind I could never have imagined. For weeks I wouldn't let anyone else hold you because I couldn't let go of you."

Posy began to sob without a sound or a tremor. Alone at the kitchen table she hung on to her coffee cup with both hands. For the first time in her life, her mother did not move to comfort her tears. She didn't say another word and returned to her suds.

After a long suffocating silence she whispered, "Can't you let me help you, mama, at least let me try."

"No, this is what I do."

"I'm not a guest mama."

She didn't respond. The conversation had come to an end. The door separating the two women had been shut, locked and bolted. Neither of them had the key.

The evening came slowly after a day of side stepping and polite nothingness. Her father and the boy were gone most of the afternoon, on purpose, she thought.

Her mother was far too busy with the laundry, talking on the phone and pulling carrots out of the ground. She felt invisible. Even the boy considered her little more than, 'be polite to company.'

After a light supper and the boy had gone to bed, she sat on the front porch watching the fireflies dance across the moonless night.

The screen door opened and her father came out and sat on the step beside her.

"When you were a kid you couldn't understand why they couldn't live in a jar," he said, looking out into the night.

"Nothing can live in a jar daddy."

"How long are you planning on staying?"

"How long do you want me to stay?"

"I wanted you to stay forever."

"You wanted me to stay a little girl forever."

"I guess I did. Remember when we went to the dance and you stood on the top of my boots and I danced you all over the floor? You were so light, I didn't even feel you there."

"I remember, I felt so grown up, like a queen."

They both fell silent. She was angry. They could look back at the good old days with affection but they could never have a conversation about the issues at hand at the moment.

"I love you daddy. Just for once look at me like I'm here, I love you. Why can't we find some adult common ground that we can meet on without the battle of the minds? I'm not a little girl anymore. I wish I was so you could be my prince charming again." The tears were close to the surface.

"You broke your mama's heart. That's my wife you hurt. I don't cotton to anyone hurting my wife, you above all."

"What about your heart?"

"I need to check on the boy." He stood up and went into the house, leaving the question a bitter sting on her tongue.

"The boy is going to grow up too daddy, in spite of you," she yelled after him.

He opened the screen door again, "By the way, there is a dance on Saturday night, Dustin's band, think it over."

She didn't want to think it over, or any other way. She didn't want to hear Dustan's music, see his face or listen to his questions, but she knew he was one of the reasons she had come back. He was on her 'unfinished business' list. Her head felt like it was in a blender set on high.

Sitting at the breakfast table on Saturday morning her father was polishing his good boots to a high black sheen. Her mother had rollers in her hair. No one mentioned the dance.

She ate her scrambled eggs trading small talk with the boy. She was tired. Her mind rattled most of the night, she couldn't sleep through the noise.

"Are you going to the dance with mama and daddy?"

"I'm not sure."

"How come?"

"I'm just tired." 'Of everything.' She thought.

"You could take a nap."

"What about you, what are you going to do?"

"I'm going to Rudy's for a sleep over." He jumped up and down.

She spent the day avoiding the thought, but as the clock brought evening closer something was seething inside of her.

She wasn't prepared for the anger she felt toward herself. She went to her room to get it out of her system. The internal chastising began; what did you expect, to come back and everything would be hunky-dory? A clean slate at every turn and everyone falling at your feet? And what about Richard? The business? What about your own changes, are you really that person that left to see what was beyond the wheat fields and the Sand Hills?

She fell on her bed and looked at the glacier blue eyes, the smile and the curls on top of his head.

"I didn't think in a million years that you would still be in the Capitol of Nowhere. Why aren't you in Nashville or somewhere?" She talked out loud to the picture.

"Are you okay in there?"

"Yeah mama, I'm fine."

"Can I come in?"

"Sure, come on in."

The door opened and her mother stood in the doorway. She had forgotten how beautiful she could be. The low cut blue dress was soft and flowing.

"You look lovely, Mama."

"Thank you dear. We are about to leave. We have to take hot-shot to Rudy's. Are you coming to the dance?"

"I don't know yet, I'm not ready anyway."

"Ok, we'll see you if we see you."

She took a shower, washed her hair and looked through the closet, choosing white jeans and a loose fitting white shirt with a pale blue T-shirt underneath. She didn't want to wear anything that suggested anything other than just covering her body.

The parking lot in front and around the Bar-X Steakhouse was packed with cars and pickups. She drove around looking for a parking space thinking she would just forget it and go home when she found one two blocks away.

She stood outside the door, taking a deep breath and clenching her fists. She could hear Dustin's voice. She opened the door and the music and blue smoke hit her in the face like a baseball bat.

She weaved her way through the bodies on the dance floor. She knew her parents would have a table in front of the stage.

He had his eyes closed singing, 'Crazy, I'm crazy for trying, crazy for crying, crazy for loving you.' Then he opened his eyes and saw her standing in front of the stage right below him. His voice cracked and he couldn't finish the next line. His hands began to shake and couldn't find the next chord on his guitar. He threw the strap of his guitar over his head, put the guitar in its stand, turned to the band and said, "Finish the set, I'm on break."

He jumped off the stage and stood looking at her in disbelief. He wasn't smiling.

"What are you still doing here?" I thought you might be in Nashville, or should be." I said.

"That's a nice thought."

"Are my parents here?"

"They're around somewhere."

"Ok, look, I suppose we should talk. When do you have to go back up there?"

"About half an hour. So now you want to talk, what brought that on after all this time?"

"I don't know. Can I buy the star a beer?"

"Sure."

They went to the bar and got one draft and one coke. Dustin looked around the room. "Let's get away from all these people and the noise. There's tables outside on the deck for that ultimate dining experience."

"How uptown."

"Yeah well, we do our best."

They sat down at one of the picnic tables. It was a beautiful clear night. They sipped their drinks trying to sooth the awkwardness of the moment.

"So, I'm not interested in chit-chat. From where I'm sitting, you owe me big time. I at least deserve to know the why's." He was close to crying.

"I never wanted to hurt you Dustin, but the truth is, I would have hurt you more by staying. I wanted something this town couldn't give me, and you were content to live your life here. It never would have worked for us and in the end I would have broken your heart more in the long run because we would have had more invested in each other. I did love you but not enough to loose myself."

She told him about her trip to Seattle, Flash, Auntie B, Hope, the business and finally about Richard. She explained that Richard was a friend, nothing more at this point.

"Wow," he said.

"That's it? That's all you have to say?"

"No, I'm just a little shocked. Why did you put yourself through all of that? You had no idea of what could have happened to you. You didn't even contact your parents. Do you have any idea how cruel that is?"

"I do now, I regret it deeply. It has been eating away at me all this time, that's one reason I'm here now."

"Are you just here to ease your own conscience?"

"No."

"I'm feeling a little selfish right now, no call, no letter, nothing. I haven't stopped loving you, not for one second and I don't want to love you anymore. You're always in my way, I can't turn around without bumping into you. I can't move forward because you're in the way."

"Why don't you get out of here and get a fresh start?"

"That's your solution, not mine. I have a son, and a life such as it is. True, he doesn't see me as his daddy, but I'm in his life and I intend to stick around and see him grow up."

"He looks like you."

He looked at his watch, "I have to go, hang around if you want." He leaned over and gave her a kiss on the cheek.

Back on stage, he picked up his guitar, adjusted the microphone, and began to sing, 'I Don't Hurt Anymore.' He looked her in the eye and sang the opening lines to her, ' I don't hurt anymore, all my teardrops are dried, no more walking the floor with this burning inside.'

She turned and walked away. She stopped by her parents'

table and gave them a quick goodbye and left.

Outside, she ran to her car. Her hands shaking so hard she could hardly put the key into the ignition. The car behind her and the one in front had her pinned in. With every forward and reverse her frustration grew. By the time she turned the wheel enough to get out of the trap tears made vision close to impossible. Thankfully, there was no traffic. They were tears of freedom and loss. She remembered what her mother had said, 'the first time only happens once.' She realized that she truly was a guest in their lives, and to one little boy, a stranger. Someone once said that you couldn't go home again. She felt an overwhelming wave of homesickness wash over her and a longing for the smell of salt air.

The next morning she awoke to the sound of voices. She looked out the window to see Dustin's van. "Oh swell," she said, throwing on jeans and a T-shirt. She went into the bathroom and looked in the mirror. She was a mess, and she didn't care.

In the kitchen she poured coffee, everyone stopped talking. There was enough tension in the air to rival Seattle fog.

She sat down at the table and looked at Dustin. "So, you're up early. Having reinforcements for breakfast?"

"No, I just want to see if we can all come to some agreement about Dusty."

Her father raised his fist over his head and slammed it down on the table with a thud that broke his coffee cup.

"Not a chance in hell am I going to upset that boy's life or let anyone else do it. Neither one of you had a place for him when he was born. Well, we did. We are the only parents he has ever known, and I don't intend for that to change, do you hear me?"

Tears came to his eyes, his face turned beet red. She had never seen her father show much emotion, let alone cry. She stood up and put her hands on his shoulders. She was frightened.

"Daddy, Dustin and I have no intention of changing that."

"What do you want then? Why now?" His red eyes bore into hers.

"I just want to make things right somehow, even though I can't fix it. I wanted to see you, mama, Dustin and Dusty. I'm going back to Seattle and I want to have you send pictures of Dusty sometimes so I can see him grow up, I want to visit sometimes and buy him ice cream cones, I want to call and hear your voice over the phone and be part of your lives. You're my parents for crying out loud. There isn't anything I can say to make you understand why I had to leave."

"That's right, nothing. Your grandma taught me about responsibility; you make your bed, you sleep in it. Your mama was brought up the same way and we tried to raise you right. What about you two?" He looked at Dustin.

"There is no 'us two' Ralph.. I will love her forever but we live in two different worlds, we don't have anything in common anymore, except for you and Dusty. That isn't about us, and it isn't enough. As sad as it is, it just isn't enough."

"I could never live up to your goodness Dustin. You loved

me too well. We were best friends before we messed it up. I wish we could be friends again."

"How do we do that?" He put his head in his hands.

"I don't know. Maybe we could stop blaming each other. All of us, maybe we could just give each other some slack. You're a good man Dustin. You have a good heart, you have the right values and you're cute as a button. There is a wonderful girl out there just waiting for you to notice her but you have to open your eyes to the possibility. When you get married call me and I'll sing at your wedding.

"That could keep me from getting married." He chuckled in spite of himself.

Her father was angry again. "Sure, let's all hug and be best friends. Is that how it works in the city? Wouldn't that just be ducky for you? You get to walk away again, off the hook."

"Shut up! Both of you shut up!" Her mother screamed. They were stunned. They looked at her, then at each other in silence. It was as if she had just thrown ice water across the room.

"Don't you see what's happening here? This might be the first time you have actually talked to each other."

"You're not much better, Mama. Dad just pretends nothing exists while you shove everything down, put on a happy face and trip the light fantastic, while I'm stuck in the middle trying to be noticed."

No one spoke for a long time until Ralph looked at her, "I have to pick up Dusty, want to ride along?"

She was surprised but pleased. They climbed into the old

pickup. The drivers seat was worn from years of Levi rivets scooting in and out. The gearshift groaned. Over the years the back had hauled kids, dogs, hay bales, milk cans, fence posts, barbed wire, saddles, chicken feed and groceries.

"She still runs good for an old girl," he smiled.

Then he was quiet. He had both hands on the steering wheel. His knuckles were white like he was holding on to something for dear life.

"You never expect your kids to grow up. It happens so slowly that it is a surprise when that day comes. You know they will leave the house but you don't expect them to leave town. You think they will be around for Sunday dinner with their kids. I should have seen it coming, always reading those magazines about those fancy people. You were always looking past the sunset. You were a dreamer, you couldn't survive here. I guess I always knew it somehow."

He had said all he could say and both of them knew it need never to be mentioned again. He had noticed, after all. Everything in her fought not to cry and the meadowlarks continued to sing.

They drove the dry road over the Sandhills, throwing a wake of dust flying behind them. The tall prairie grass was green in spite of the lack of rain. Antelope grazed without alarm. They raised their heads only as an acknowledgement.

He pulled over to the side of the road and rolled down the window.

"Listen," he whispered.

"To what?"

"To nothing."

They let the silence engulf them for awhile.

"Nebraska isn't a place Dad, it's a way of being and it doesn't get lost when you cross the state line."

"There are a lot of state lines between here and Seattle."

"It's in my heart, no matter where I go. You could come to Seattle to visit, I'll show you the ocean."

"Do they have antelope in Seattle?"

"No, they have trees and mountains and water."

"They have traffic, rain and too many people."

"Not everywhere."

"Well, we'll see sometime. Best get Dusty now."

He turned onto the road to the sprawling cattle ranch. Dusty came running up the road to meet them. His oversized cowboy hat flew off his head. He picked it up, slapped it across his knee and put it back on his head. She had seen her dad do that so many times. That one small innocent act was an arrow through her heart and at that moment she knew that he was her father's son and it would never be otherwise. It was also clear that she couldn't slip and call her father 'Dad' in front of the boy.

"Hey daddy," he shouted.

"Hey Hot Shot, did you have a good time?"

"Sure did. Rudy and I found a snake in the ditch, it wasn't a rattlesnake though. They wouldn't let us keep it. We had cake for dinner and I road the pony for a while."

They went to the house to pick up Dusty's bag. Ralph talked to Rudy's parents for awhile while the boys ran around one more time.

Posy stayed in the pickup, knowing she was close to the time when she would be leaving. She wondered if she should stay for the birthday party. Maybe it would be better if they had the day free of her. Besides, Dustin would be there. She didn't know, she would ask her mother. She wanted to give him a present.

She remembered the day he was born. Her mother was wrong, she did love him. He was so small and fuzzy. He scared her to death.

They opened the driver's door and he scooted in beside her. When Ralph got into the seat Dusty said, "Can I drive daddy?"

"Sure, hop over here."

He got onto Ralph's lap, grabbed the steering wheel and began to maneuver the pickup down the road, with Ralph having his foot on the gas.

"Move over son, you're taking up the whole road."

She watched the two of them. Dusty was so like her dad and yet he looked more like Dustin than her.

He drove all the way home. Her mother was hanging sheets on the clothesline when they arrived. Nothing like the smell of line-dried sheets, she thought.

Dusty jumped off Ralph's lap and ran to share his excitement, "Hey mama, I drove all the way home and I didn't hit anything."

"Hey yourself, aren't you a big boy," she said with pride in her voice.

"Can I help, I want to talk to you."

"Sure, that would be nice."

She took a wet sheet out of the basket, folded it over the line and secured it with clothespins.

"Nice breeze today. What are the birthday plans?" She asked her mother.

"Thought we could have a picnic at the park, have a few people over."

"Mama, you never have just a few people over," she laughed.

Her mother laughed back, "Well, you can't invite one without the other."

"So you mean most of the valley."

"Always seems to work out that way. There will be some of your old friends. You haven't called any of them, they will be so glad to see you. They would be hurt if they knew you were here and didn't contact them."

"What about Dustin?"

"Of course. For what it's worth, I really want you to stay for the party. Wilma will be so glad to see you. She is all crippled up with arthritis now but she keeps going, bless her heart."

"Will you go with me to get a present?"

"What do you have in mind?"

"I was thinking about a saddle."

"That's too grand. We don't buy him fancy presents very often, and coming from you wouldn't be right. We'll get him fitted for a saddle when he gets older and won't out grow it."

"Ok, boots maybe?"

"That would be better."

The days before the party became increasingly hectic. Ralph and Dusty found anything to do to keep out of the way. The phone rang off the hook, people stopped by and food multiplied in the kitchen at a rapid rate. Cakes, pies and salads were on every flat surface.

Posy was thankful that her mother finally gave in and bought a chicken at the grocery store. She wouldn't have to spend the day on plucking duty. She hated the smell of boiling hot wet feathers.

Her mother grumbled every time she turned the chicken in the pan, "Just doesn't taste the same and it's so expensive and store bought eggs, wouldn't have the darn things in the house. I just have laying hens for that reason."

Posy and her mother took an afternoon to go to town for lunch out and to shop for Dusty. Posy found black, hand tooled boots, black like her dad's. Her mother bought Wranglers, a shirt and Lincoln Logs.

They sat in a booth at the only café in town. They ate in silence until the pie came.

"You're leaving soon, aren't you?" Her mother asked, sipping her iced tea.

"After the party, after he opens his presents. There will be people around and besides I don't want to leave from the house."

"I suppose that would be best for everybody. That means I won't be able to fall apart in public. Just slip away when you can, I'm not good with 'good-byes'. I'm glad you came. I know it hasn't been easy but it was for the good for all of us. I know your father appreciates it, even though he won't admit it."

"Mama, thank you for what you have done for Dusty and for allowing Dustin to be around him. If I still have a job or a home when I get back to Seattle, I want to help out with the expenses."

"That isn't necessary dear."

"It would make me happy if I could help out."

"We can cross that bridge when we get to it," she smiled, reaching into her purse and taking out an envelope. She handed it to Posy.

Inside the envelope was a 5x7 photo of Dusty looking into the camera with a big smile.

"It's this years school picture. You can have it. I can send more when they are taken."

"Thank you so much, I will treasure this always."

The day before the party Posy called the Airline and cancelled her flight. She called the Rent-a-car Company and said that she would turn in the car in Seattle. She packed the trunk while the family went to the grocery store.

Dusty was so excited he couldn't eat supper and bedtime was impossible. He was up and down the stairs several times.

Ralph gave in and said to him, "come here son, grab that afghan on your way."

Dusty came to Ralph, curled up on his lap and disappeared under the mound of wool. Ralph whispered in his ear,

"If you don't go to sleep you will be too tired to have fun tomorrow. Now close your eyes and don't think about anything."

Posy kissed her dad on the forehead and went to bed. Before she knew it, morning had come. She didn't open her eyes. It was his day and not one year did this day come that she didn't think of him so hard that she thought something in her would burst. She loved him, yet she couldn't understand why she didn't have that 'mother thing' that mothers are supposed to have. It came so natural for some people. Her mother would scoop up anything that landed on the doorstep, human or other wise and she was bonded for life. And there was always food; food just seemed to happen without anyone being in the kitchen. She was something all right, just ask anyone within a hundred miles.

She opened her eyes, took a deep breath and swung her legs over the edge of her bed. She sat there for a moment filling her with the feeling of this room that had been a refuge over so many bumps and bruises.

She made the bed and dressed in jeans and the red blouse with fringe on the sleeves that she found in her closet. It had been her mother's favorite and she smiled when she walked in the kitchen. She asked her dad if he wanted to play a game of Crib. He was delighted to take her on; it was the one thing that brought them head to head on common ground. At the last of the game she was ahead until he pegged twelve holes and passed with great vibrato.

"Well, well, look at that, the champ still holds the title," he laughed as he put the peg in the last hole.

The park was crowded when they got there. Picnic tables were placed end to end; food was lined according to category. Salads of every combination were first. Every household had their own recipe of potato salad and everyone brought one, boasting that theirs was the best in the valley. The same was said about the deviled eggs, baked beans and fried chicken. The dessert table was last, loaded with chocolate cakes, pies, bread pudding, tapioca pudding and every color of Jell-O. Coolers full of beer and pop were everywhere.

The men sat in the shade under the hundred year old Elm trees playing poker or cribbage. Some pitched horseshoes or threw baseballs. The women caught up on their lives and kids ran everywhere or played on the swings and teeter-totters.

Posy was received, as was predictable, as if she had only gone to the market. There was no fanfare, no explosion of emotion, and just a quiet acceptance. There were hugs and smiles.

Her high school friends acted like they had seen her yesterday. There were giggles, hugs and warm smiles. Some had aged more than others. They sat at a table away from the gathered crowd, eight females talking at the same time. They discussed the good old days; laughing at being caught crawling out the bedroom window when they had been grounded in the first place, the night they first smoked a cigarette that they had stolen from their dad's pack, and how they thought they were going to die for sure. They bragged about their kids, trying to one-up each story of how perfect their little darling was. They talked about the Homecoming Queen marrying the Homecoming King. They had fallen in love dancing to the music of the Everly Brothers, and then created their heir to the throne in the parking lot the night of the homecoming dance.

She couldn't have said that her son was the cutest and the smartest of all. No one had known she was pregnant. There had been a few faint remarks that she was becoming 'a little chubby.' After awhile she refused invitations, making excuses to avoid the comments on her swelling belly. They all thought the family had taken a long vacation that summer, when in fact, they had gone to stay with her mother's sister in Omaha while they waited for the baby to come. When they got home, the whole valley thought her parents had lost their minds when they adopted and brought home an infant.

Tired of playing 'remember when' when in fact she didn't remember at all, Posy walked around the park giving greetings to some of the elderly folks that she knew from childhood.

Dustan was sitting against a tree playing his acoustic. She stood behind him listening, then moved in front of him and sat down beside him.

"You are the music, you know?"

"Am I a sharp or a flat?" They both laughed.

"Life is easy here in a way, it's just not too complicated."

"That's true, it seems to roll on from one generation to the next, there is something oddly safe about that. I had to learn how to survive in a different world where easy doesn't always come easy. I have gone from eating half-rotten food, because that's all there was, to being able to afford steak. Every moment in between was a challenge of adjusting. I don't know any other way anymore; I had to come home to understand that. I want my life to fit like a pair of well worn jeans."

"I don't understand because I don't have the contrast. I have always been content with what I know." His eyes looked around at the familiar faces.

"There is nothing wrong with that and I respect you for knowing who you are and where you belong. There is a whole world of people that can't say that."

"Can you say that?"

"Almost," she smiled. She got up, kissed him and walked away. He didn't move or call after her.

She saw her mother putting candles on the three-layer lemon cake that was Dusty's favorite.

"I'm going to stay to watch him open his presents," she said.

"That's good, I'm glad you changed your mind."

Her mother called everyone to come as she put the wrapped gifts beside the cake. Dusty was the first to get there, running so fast that he almost tripped over his own feet. He opened all of his gifts, saving the ones from Posy and Dustin until the last.

He ripped the paper from the box, opened the lid and yelled, "Boots, daddy, look they are just like yours."

He gently took them out of the box, took off his shoes and pulled them onto his feet. He strutted around looking down at them. He gave Posy a big hug and thanked her over and over again.

She felt his little body next to hers and smelled his hair and that split second was worth anything she had to endure to get to that place.

He opened Dustin's present and found a baseball glove inside. He put it on his hand and said, "What a most excellent birthday."

After the candles had been blown out and the cake eaten, she helped her mother clean up the wrappings and paper plates.

People began to wander around, children full of sugar were back to their playing. Dustin took the boy out to the open space and showed him how to hit the center of his glove with his fist to soften up the spot where the ball should go. He threw the ball slowly and low. Dusty squealed and raised his arm, the ball in his glove.

Her steps toward her father were slow. He was pitching horseshoes and it was his turn. She sadly stood watching him. He was more bent over than the arrow straight man she had known, but his eyes were keen and his aim was sure.

"Daddy, I have to go now."

He didn't look at her. He brought the horseshoe up to his face, sighted the pin, threw and missed.

"Daddy, I have to go now. I love you."

He still didn't look at her, but she thought she heard him say under his breath, 'love you' as he kicked a stone and looked down.

She turned and walked away feeling like a horseshoe had

hit her in the stomach. Something in her knew that she would never see him again. She was gripped with a sad emptiness she had never known before.

Her mother was standing a distance away watching. She went to her.

"I'll walk you to the car."

They stood holding each other. Her mother clung to her sobbing. At last she pulled away and looked her in the eye.

"I love you dear, have a safe journey home."

Posy nodded, got in the car and drove away, not able to see the street through the blur. She didn't look back.

She stopped the car at the only stop sign in town that split the street with no name and the East, West highway. There was no real reason to stop but she sat in front of the sign, knowing her right turn would be final.

A large brown paper bag on the passenger side floor caught her eye. She smiled before she opened it. She knew something good was inside. No one ever left her mom's sight without arms full of food containers. She would go to the local Tupperware parties and buy more than one of everything offered so she could fill them for leaving company. There were piles of the containers in the basement; no one ever left the house hungry. She opened the bag and looked inside, sure enough.

She looked to the left at miles of empty highway, turned the wheel to the right and pointed the car toward the north and west.

She chose Montana rather than the endless brown landscape, the dust and the miles of one truck after another on Southern Wyoming's Interstate 80.

Just across the Nebraska, Wyoming border into Torrington she pulled into a rest stop. She had driven for several hours and was hungry, stiff and anxious to retaste the home cooking resting in the sack. She realized her mother had taken the empty Tupperware to the picnic and filled them there. She shook her head and laughed. The apple doesn't fall far from the tree, she thought.

She took the sack to a nearby picnic table and spread out the containers. She opened the lids and found deviled eggs, three kinds of potato salad, fried chicken, two different kind of chocolate cake, a piece of peach pie and a thermos of coffee. She took out a paper plate, plastic utensils and dished up a bit of everything. A family walked by, looked at the food, at her and then at each other.

She packed up and hit the road again. As she approached Casper the sun was going down. She was exhausted when she saw the Holiday Inn sign.

She checked in and tried to adjust to not being in motion. As soon as she was in her room she turned on the bath water. When her back and legs were limber again she went for a walk around the building, went back to her room and turned on the Television. She thought it wise to finish all of the potato salad before it went bad.

It was just dawn when she was in the office filling her thermos and paying her bill.

Interstate 25 connected to Interstate 90 going to Montana, then west to Spokane. She was inching closer. Montana truly was big sky country and the sky was a pure blue with tall white thunderclouds that never produced rain. The wide-open spaces were at least dotted with hills and mountains. The pine trees were becoming thicker and greener on the hills that banked along the highway. The crystal clear river was flowing rapidly and boiling over the rocks. The traffic was almost non-existent. She felt wonderfully alone.

The second morning she was on the road by five o'clock. The light hit the tops of the hills, and got brighter and lower as she drove along the river.

Suddenly she saw a green sign; Custer Battlefield—Next Right. She hadn't known where it was exactly but had always wanted to see it.

The wide paved entrance going up a hill was void of traffic. The bus parking area was empty. There were no cars in the parking lot.

She parked in front of the Visitors' Center that was to open in an hour. She followed the path that led to the overlook of the valley and the Little Big Horn River.

The tall silver grass swayed in random patches. It moved back and forth then quit while another patch moved. There was no breeze, no reason for the movement on the ground. She stood in the heavy stillness, watching, almost seeing ghosts on horseback moving the grass with their hoofs.

The history books came to life as she imagined riders descending the behind the river below, descending to fight one more battle.

Directly in front of her, scattered randomly, small white tombstones rose above the grass, almost as if they were placed where the wounded had fallen. Off to the side, by itself, a black tombstone belonging to Custer. The warm morning sun beat on her back, yet she had the chills. One lone meadowlark sang.

She didn't know how long she had stood there but when she returned to the Visitor Center people were beginning to arrive. The Center was open. She went inside and in the middle of the lobby; in a glass case was a mannequin wearing Custer's blue uniform. She was amazed at how small the man had been. He couldn't have been much over five feet tall and with a very thin build. The irony was too much for her.

She was somber as she returned to the highway. The miles and hours disappeared under her wheels. She was soon equidistant from her past and her uncertain future. She began to contemplate what was ahead. She knew Hope would be less than receptive at the sight of her. Then there was Richard, what was she going to do about him? With Nebraska resolved, could she look at him now as being something beyond friendship, would he even let her?

The flat barren landscape of Eastern Washington was making her sleepy. It was dusk. She would spend the night in Moses Lake and be in Seattle tomorrow.

It was the day of reckoning and she knew she was on the way to the rest of her life. She was on the road before sun up. She drove fast while the road was flat and open before it began the incline over the Cascade Range.

Her apprehension increased as she dropped down the west summit of Steven's pass. She opened the windows and filled her lungs with the sweet smell of cedar trees and a hint of salt air.

EPILOGUE

Despite my efforts to stay awake, I had lost the battle. Perhaps I had worn myself out and the soft warm purr of the kitten had lulled me over the edge. The traffic above had subsided to an occasional thump. It was increasingly cold and somehow I had slipped away.

A faint hint of light came through the cracks of the box flaps. Traffic was building above me so it must be the beginning of rush hour.

My stomach growled, demanding to be fed. It was out of luck, the tuna sandwich was long gone.

Every bone, every muscle was frozen in the fetal position. I had to try to unfold myself. Every attempt hurt everything. The kitten crawled out from my armpit, yawned and began to wash its face.

Think of it as taking off a Band-Aid, I thought, do it quickly. I scooted until my feet and knees were out of the box. I stretched my legs until I was unfolded and could stand. Every part of me began to cramp and spasm.

By now it was daylight. I was running in circles to force blood to flow into my legs when I heard his voice from a distance away.

"Hope, is that you?"

I turned around and saw Flash standing there with his hands on his hips. I hardly recognized him. He had filled out, no longer skinny and gaunt. His hair was short and his cloths were clean and well matched.

"Flash?"

"Flash in the flesh,' he flashed that big smile of his.

"Well, don't you just look fabulous. Where have you been?"

"I went to the mission after mama died and I'm still there, on a working basis. I'm a counselor and loving it. I guess in some way I'm carrying on what mama started. And guess what? I met the most wonderful girl and she married me, can you believe anyone would want to marry me?"

"Yes I can, she's a smart girl, I'm so proud of you."

"I come here from time to time. I never see the same people twice, it's more transient that it used to be but I come for me, some things are not easy to forget. What are you doing here anyway?"

"I came looking for something."

"Did you find it?"

"Yes, I did."

I told him about what had happened since Auntie Bea had died and I told him that Posy had taken off for parts unknown.

"That's quite amazing. So you're a big time businesswoman and artist now, I'm not surprised. It does surprise me that

Posy left like that, she must have had a good reason."

"I'm just perplexed, I haven't heard from her at all."

"How are you doing?"

"I'm doing ok, I work, now I work twice as hard.

A horn honked in mid thought. He was early. I wanted more time with Flash, and there were too many things to say.

"Who's that?" Flash asked.

"My ride."

Burke jumped out of the car and came running over to us with concern on his face.

"Are you ok? Who are you?" He turned to Flash.

"Burke, this is my good friend Flash. Lighten up."

"Are you ready to go?" Burke ignored the introduction.

I fell into Flash's arms. We held each other like hanging on to an old sweet memory. We vowed to keep in touch but knew we probably wouldn't.

"I'm ready now," I said, and I was.

I picked up my backpack and a meow came softly from the inside.

"What on earth is that?" Burke asked.

"A kitten, it adopted me, I belong to it."

"What a ploy."

"Thank you, it's going to live at the studio."

"Why?"

"Because I don't want Apollo to get jealous and beat up on it."

"Hope, Apollo is a miniature Pomeranian, how much damage can he do?"

"He may be small, but he has a Doberman attitude."

We got into the car and I looked to see Flash but he had gone.

"Where do you want to go, home or the studio?"

"Home, I want to take a shower and change, I'll be back to the studio in a couple of hours."

"Was it worth it?" He asked.

"I don't know, ask me next week," I said rubbing my leg.

Depleted and hungry, Burke opened the front door and saw Veronica's worried face.

"Where have you been? Not that I have to ask."

"I spent the night in my car. I couldn't just dump Hope there and come home."

She put her arms around his waist. "That doesn't surprise me."

"I really need a shower." He pulled away and for an instant his eyes went blank.

Veronica heard the shower as she put bread in the toaster and scrambled eggs just as he liked them. She reflected that she had seen that look on Burke's face before, but this time he didn't have his office as a fortress.

Shirtless and barefoot he shuffled into the kitchen like an old man whose legs had forgotten how to make steps. He plopped down on his chair at the table and devoured his breakfast with as few bites as possible.

With only a glance at him, Veronica made herself busy at the sink. When he pushed the empty plate aside she sat across from him, taking his hands in hers.

He looked at the comfort of her hands holding his. "From time to time one of the girls mentioned Auntie Bea or someone from the streets, but it was just in passing. I didn't pay much attention. It was a world I didn't understand and the truth is I didn't want to.

"Last night I was parked across the street where I could keep an eye on Hope. I was sitting on the leather seats of my car with the keys in the ignition in case I wanted to turn on the heater or the radio. I sat there, staring at the box in the darkness.

"I couldn't see anything but the box. She was in there on the cold ground. I didn't know what was going on in that flimsy shelter. Was she scared? Cold? Hungry? Crying? What? I didn't know and there was nothing I could do." He groaned with pain.

Veronica got up and walked around the kitchen only to sit down again. "Burke, we all live in our own box. Some are grand. Some are barely held together and the rest are somewhere in between. No one knows what goes on in someone else's box, even when we are invited in for awhile."

He shook his head. "Maybe we are all just isolated. What a shame."

"What would you want to say to Auntie Bea if she were here?" Veronica forced a smile.

"Nothing. I would just want to listen."

"You're not isolated anymore, Burke."

"Neither are you."

I limped into my office and began to adjust my head. I

had stopped at the pet store and bought a litter box and cat food. I put the box and a plate of food under the drawing table and showed my new nemesis where to do what it had to do from both ends.

The phone rang just as someone knocked on my door. I picked up the phone, "Hello, this is Hope."

"Come in," I yelled at the door.

I looked up and saw Posy walking in the door. She wasn't smiling, and there was a tinge of fear on her face.

"I'm going to have to call you back," I said into the receiver and hung up the phone.

"What are you doing here?" My tone was less than friendly. I was in shock.

"I thought I would fill out a job application," she tried to smile.

"What? You are kidding, right? You had a job and you threw it away leaving me to clean up your mess. Cut and run isn't in our job description, so we don't have any openings right now."

The longer I talked, the angrier I was becoming. I knew if I didn't shut up it was going to get ugly. I got up and looked out the window. There was a tense silence filling the room.

I turned around, "Come here, look at those buildings down there. That's a constant reminder of where I was not so long ago. I look at that every day and know I could still be walking those streets. I went back to the viaduct last night and spent the night in a cardboard box, right where Auntie Bea's chair used to be. I was alone, there were only the sounds of traffic and the memories in my head."

"I don't blame you for being mad, I expected it and I deserve it. I would appreciate it if you would just put it aside and listen to me for a little while. Can we have some coffee please?"

"You know where it is."

"I really don't want to go down there."

"Chicken! I'll be right back."

I went to the lunchroom to get the coffeepot and Veronica was washing out the cups from yesterday.

"Did I see Posy walking up the stairs, or have I lost my mind?"

"She is in my office, I don't know where this is going."

I sat the cups and the coffeepot on my desk and she began to tell me about her journey. She reached into her purse and put a 5x7 photo of a beautiful little boy in front of me. I held my breath as I stared at the face that was Posy's reflection.

"That's my son."

I couldn't speak; I was limp and clammy. All I could do was to look at that face in disbelief.

"I had to go while I had the nerve. I knew if I talked to any of you I wouldn't be able to go, that someone would try to talk me out of it. I didn't want to explain something that I wasn't sure of yet. How stupid would it have sounded if I said, 'I have to go find myself' even though it was true."

"Give me one good reason why we should take you back?"

Picking up the photo and looking at it, Elizabeth said,

"Give me one good reason why you shouldn't?"

Before I could respond, the kitten jumped up on my lap. It lay down, began to purr and lick its paws. The words I had first said to it echoed back to me, "I was a stray once and someone took me in."

I looked at my watch, then at Posy. "Have you had lunch?"

"No."

As we had so many times before, we stood together on the sidewalk in silence, and then crossed the street to the nearest restaurant.

ISBN 1425180195-1